Blue Black Water

The Sinking of the *C. M. Demson*

R O N   M A Y

PAGE PUBLISHING, INC.
Conneaut Lake, PA

First originally published by Page Publishing 2020

ISBN 978-1-64334-811-7 (pbk)
ISBN 978-1-64334-809-4 (hc)
ISBN 978-1-64334-810-0 (digital)

Printed in the United States of America

DEDICATION

· · · · · · · ● ● ● ● ● ● ● · · · · ·

*Y*ou are the best!

      I want my children and my grandchildren to have a perspective on what makes a good story worth telling. I have fabricated this fictional tale with as much realism and connection to real events as I could. Taking the effort to read this novel will lead to an understanding of our family's history. This is simply a few-month segment of my life, but it was a significant summer for me and a terrific backdrop to tell the young man's experience of naivete, adventure, and character. The principles I describe in this story are important. I believe that if you can live these principles, your life can be a bit more magical.

      I dedicate this work to Christine Denise Lambert May. Thank you for being my partner for over forty-six years, longer than we have been married. You have helped me graduate from engineering school, progress through my career, be a better father and grandfather, and most of all, show me how to love life. You are the best!

C O N T E N T S

FOREWORD

Richard Hemsley is a business leader with over thirty years' experience within and outside financial services. Whilst from a modest background, with no college education, Richard rose to be COO of the world's largest bank, led the United Kingdom's largest asset finance business, and held a number of board-level positions before retiring. He has led many tens of thousands of people from across the world and across cultures. He has delivered both growth and turnaround strategies for businesses during his career and has had the opportunity to learn from good and not-so-good leaders. His philosophy, based on these experiences, is that the core set of skills that a leader needs are common and have been invaluable in times of business change and challenge as well as within his personal life.

So I find it a little ironic and perhaps frightening that I am starting to write this short piece from a vehicle ferry somewhere in the middle of the English Channel on a stormy October evening. Perhaps I could not have chosen a more appropriate time and location! However, as with all the very best experiences in life, and as with leadership, you have to live it to understand it!

Any book that claims to address the subject of leadership must have real, tangible stories at its core to ensure we, as readers, can understand the theory in real-life situations and to ensure that the learning has a greater chance of being embedded within us. In part, this is why many colleges and business schools use case studies as a teaching method—the real stories. However, this book is unique in how it blends together a number of real-life events to give us all insights into how leadership works and how it does not work.

The ability to lead people and be seen as a leader is a set of special skills which is not the domain of a privileged few, but one which we all possess. However, few of us will grow to excel as leaders and even less really take the time and make the effort to develop those basic capabilities we already have. In my experience, which is largely based on thirty years in the cut and thrust of the corporate world, this is because all too often the arrogance of our limited corporate success allows the so-called leaders to assume they have mastered these most complex set of skills. Later, they, or more likely the people that are being led by them, find out that the only real talent lay in management which, as I will cover later, is not leadership.

Before we dive into this story, I want to ensure you are always on the lookout to learn from good leadership. Be aware of poor leadership as well and learn from those people and situations. Very few people who tell you they are good leaders actually turn out to be one. In fact, over my career, some of the best leaders were those who rose within a business to near the top, but very seldom became the top executive. Often, they would become part of the senior management team, perhaps a number two or running a major subsidiary but seldom the CEO. The CEO was often the strongest performance manager, a different but important skill set. Strong performance management is reflected in the blind drive for short-term profit and stock-price growth. These attributes absolutely dominated the late 1990s and early part of this century. I am not convinced it has altogether subsided, but these should not be ultimate role models for leaders of the twenty-first century.

Almost by definition, great leaders have to show humility because they need to question themselves and be open to change in themselves as reflected by different situations, different cultures, and different demands from every new set of circumstances. Never assume that what has worked in the past will work again in the future. Be ready to constantly change yourself as your leadership journey starts. It will be the most exciting journey and the most challenging of your life, and it never ends!

Of course, as with everything in leadership, my opinion is just that—an opinion based on my experiences. And the reason we should always be open to developing our leadership skills is that we all have different experiences to learn from. For example, great leaders can and do rise to the top despite my earlier observation. The impression on others that real leaders leave will last a lifetime; they have with me. And perhaps more importantly, as you start your leadership journey, you will need to appreciate that, as a leader, you will have an emotional impact on all those people around you. Make it a positive one.

Your leadership journey will be constantly demanding, and you need to be prepared for those key moments that will test if you are strong enough not to compromise on your principles and what you have learned to achieve success. Will you be ready to stick to your beliefs and knowledge if it means you will risk that next career promotion or frustrates the senior management team? Will you compromise who you are and what you stand for, or will you develop your own playbook that others come to respect and understand?

Think long and hard about what you want to be as a leader and how you want to be seen. At times in my career, I have both compromised my beliefs and held firm to them under pressure. There is only one path, the latter, which I look back on with some pride and feel good about the things I did, how I treated other people, the decisions I took, and how I developed.

So what is it that I want to say within this foreword about leadership? I think that can be distilled in to just two areas; a few words about the author and to share some of what I believe are the most important capabilities a leader must have.

Let me start by talking a little about my time with the author. We were thrust together almost twenty years ago when both arriving at business school. Not at the beginning of our leadership journeys but halfway through. At a time and a place when we didn't understand why, and in my case how, we had been relatively successful or if we were really anything beyond good or lucky managers.

It soon was clear to my classmates and me that, in the author, we had met one of those few very special people in the world who could actually claim to be a leader and someone who would leave a lasting positive impact on your life. Someone who was always willing to spend time supporting and developing others and in building their capability and confidence. Through his own humility shone a determination to be better. A drive that must have always pushed him to develop his skills in a search for improvement in all that he did.

Underpinning this drive was a hidden strength which I have seen on a number of occasions as a foundation for leadership success. Having a real understanding, a detailed understanding of how a business works and the daily challenges that the people face. It ensures that leadership is grounded in a understanding of what decisions will really mean for those people who have to turn them into reality. This results in leadership that is grounded in respect from the bottom of the organization and not just at the top.

This leads me to say something about the author that is the final, true test of leadership. The ability to take on a challenge, indeed create it, shape the journey, deliver, and have the people walking beside you at the start, during, and at the end of the journey.

Finally, in doing all this, our author has found the time to give back—give back to his local community, to his college, and to all of us. Writing this book is no small investment of time and emotion. He is a coach, a source of good council, a friend, and above all, a world-class leader.

Enough about the author. Hopefully I have convinced you that when he seeks to put pen to paper and share his thoughts and experiences, we should all pay attention. My experiences, as I have already stated, tend to come from corporate life, not the intense and genuinely life-threatening events of this book. However, I do believe there are common factors which are constant regardless of circumstances but which all leaders need to be aware of and use to ensure that any journey, over the waves or through the jungle of corporate life, is successful.

My first, and perhaps most important reflection, is that leadership has to be about change. Often you will hear leadership referred to as a journey, but it is so much more than that and so much more complex. It is about taking people and an organization on a quest that you initiate and shape for a better outcome. As such, there are a number of key elements to achieving this and being a capable individual to lead it.

You must understand where the journey that you will be leading people on will end. What does the satisfactory conclusion of the change look like? Is it an expedition into a region of unexplored jungle and success is getting safely to and from that area? Is it climbing a mountain and returning to base camp? Is it leading the launch of a new product line for a manufacturing business? The journey can have many different dimensions to it, but you, as the leader, must be clear and able to articulate what the completed journey will look like.

As you start any journey, you must have an understanding of the broad route you will follow. This can vary considerably in detail, but you must be able to convince those you lead that, whilst the goal you are setting is stretching, there is a credible route by which it can be achieved. Your specific leadership environment and the culture of the team or business you are working within will, in part, dictate the depth of plan you will need at the start of the journey.

The ability to articulate what success will look like is critical to engaging others, the people you will lead, on the journey. You must be able to paint a compelling picture and rationale for change to enable people to become passionate about the journey. After all, any change will be as important for those being led as for the leader themselves.

As you create the momentum toward a goal, a journey, then create discomfort with the present. Explain why the adventure is worth the risk, why the business cannot stand still, why things must change. Storytelling is the most engaging way of creating a desire to change. But make it personal if you can. Ensure that people believe in you, that you have understood the change, and that you are committed to it.

What I can almost guarantee is that if the journey is challenging, if the change is substantial, and if achievement of the goal will take weeks, months, or even years, then the plan will change. We all know we can take Interstate 94 from Chicago to Detroit, but even Google Maps can't always predict what lies ahead on the busy interstate.

Understanding things will go wrong or need to change, being able to accept this, replan, and move on while maintaining momentum is a critical role that leaders have to play. That doesn't mean that obstacles are not challenging; it doesn't mean that changing course should become easy or regular. It means that, occasionally, even the most detailed and comprehensive plans have to adjust to reflect unforeseen circumstances or a change in the environment in which the change is being made.

So setting a challenge of a new goal and creating the momentum and engagement for that change within any form of organization is the most important role a leader can play. Leading! And in my experience, to gain engagement, you must have an understanding of the journey and you must want to seek support, input, and challenge from those key people around you who will make the change happen.

I was once fortunate enough to be the leader at the United Kingdom's largest asset finance business. It was a one-hundred-year-old business that had grown to a dominant position in the United Kingdom market. In more recent years, growth had stalled. The business had a very experienced salesforce that covered the United Kingdom, but they were at capacity. The business needed to retain its core strengths whilst changing to reflect the ways that their customers worked in the modern business world—more technology and less face-to-face contact.

I was so excited by the challenge and opportunity to turn this business around that I took a career downward step to lead this company. I found it one of the most rewarding periods of my career. I worked very hard to put into practice many of the leadership skills I had picked up from others. I also learnt so much from those around me as we shaped plans and started the journey. Someone in my very early leadership career once said to me, "Only ever seek to lead a business where you can make a real difference." How true this was for this opportunity.

I knew very little about the asset finance industry I had stepped into, but I understood strategy and how to build a winning position. I created a small team of the most dynamic people from within the business, those who could bring fresh thinking forward and would be ready to lead the journey once we had decided which course to take. I took them away from their day jobs to work through the new strategy.

Each week, we would take our thinking back to my incumbent management team. These individuals were massively experienced in the industry and were able to challenge our thinking. What emerged over the following weeks was that the most cynical old warhorses around the management table were the most valuable. Valuable in forcing us to get our thinking right as they would expose any gaps, but ultimately, they were the most valuable because, as they were so regularly involved in the strategy as it developed, they slowly bought in to the change, the journey. The cynics became the champions.

Creating momentum and managing execution was then much more achievable as people from across the business could see an engaged and bought-in management team. Now it wasn't as simply as I have just made it seem; that would be a whole new book. But the message of creating the vision, setting out the journey, and engage-ment of key players (champions and cynics) I hope is clear enough.

On to my second key message about leadership and that is that leadership and management are two very different things, and lots of supposed leaders get this massively confused and out of balance. The first thing to acknowledge is that both are important, and as a leader, you will need to be capable in both.

As we have already discussed, the leadership role is about iden-tifying that new goal, setting out the journey, and ensuring your team is as equally committed and engaged as you are. It doesn't mean doing all the detailed thinking and planning.

I recall a period immediately after the global financial crisis in 2008 when I was COO at a very large financial institution with a global business. We had been hit very hard by the crisis and, in order to survive, needed to take cost out of the business quickly. What was ultimately delivered was the most significant cost-saving pro-gram a financial services business had ever achieved £2bn of annual run costs were taken out of the business. In first setting and then delivering this strategy, I did not set out every initiative or each step of the plans required. I brought together my leadership team. We agreed some key initiatives and the savings they would deliver based on experience. I also agreed a timeline and *rules* for things we would and would not be prepared to do to achieve the goals set.

A small group of key individuals from across the business was then asked to build the detailed plans required to deliver the initiatives and to stand up the project teams required to deliver the plans. Each week I would review progress, challenge, and make decisions as required. Mostly, however, I would be on the road talking to the many thousands of people who would be impacted by the strategy about the change that was coming, why it was required, and how it would impact them. And most important of all, I answered all and any questions they had—openly and honestly.

The program was delivered, the bank survived, and for less investment than originally estimated and within a shorter timescale. Setting and agreeing to the goal, ensuring delivery, and communicating and engaging those impacted in the need for change is leadership. Building and executing detailed implementation plans for delivery is largely management.

Management is the day-by-day, week-by-week monitoring and decision-making required to ensure the strategy remains on track. It is dominated by information and data that is required to track progress, ensuring the ship remains on the right course and isn't heading for the rocks. Management is about ensuring that legal and compliance requirements are being met and that financial and other areas of performance are in line with expectations and, where required, any recovery actions are agreed and executed. That is management—very, very important but not leadership.

As a leader, you will need to lead and manage but never get confused between the two and always think about the balance that is needed to achieve your goals and objectives. When you get to lead, you will probably have pulled together a team you believe are the right group for your journey; don't then take away the very essence of their drive by overmanaging them.

The worst "leaders" are those that are in leadership positions but actually only have management skills. Twice in my career, I have worked for two such individuals, and on both occasions, they have proven to be the most challenging and least rewarding of times. The "leaders" were very intelligent individuals and had relied on this capability for a significant period of their careers. They had, therefore, concluded they were more capable than any of those around them, resulting in them making all decisions, devaluing even very senior individuals, and in effect, becoming a full-time super manager.

A key capability of a leader is an understanding that you aren't and don't have to be the best at everything; that is why you develop or select a great team to be around you! And indeed, to allow that team to grow, to become more capable leaders in themselves, you must encourage the team to make decisions and learn for themselves how to lead.

Sometimes it can take a long time to learn you don't have to be, and never will be, perfect, and indeed, some people never have the courage to accept this point. I took too long and spent many years in my early and mid-career thinking I had to be the best in all that came across my desk. It took me far too long to learn that part of being a leader is about how you bring together a team, use the skills and experience they have, and allow them to grow. The more you can focus on helping others grow, the more you grow yourself.

Somewhat fortunately, I ended up mid-career working for a guy who was superb in this area of leadership. He was taking a key business through the most radical change in a generation. He pulled together a new leadership team of hungry individuals with different skills, different personalities, and different life experiences. I was part of that team. He knew this collection of young, aspiring leaders would make his life tough, with challenges to overcome, conflicts to be averted, and careers to be shaped. He gave those new leaders space to create their own journeys but, with just enough coaching to ensure the ship, overall, remained on the right course. In essence, he allowed the leaders to grow, to gain valuable experience, and to start to reach their potential.

I look back now and wish I had been able to learn more quickly on how to take this risk and to select and develop future talent in the way this leader did. And I look with admiration at the success this team have achieved in their subsequent careers. Other than on this page, I am not sure that his success will ever be acknowledged in the way it should be but the perfect example of leading, not managing.

If you drop into constant management, your team will find it disengaging. It will be seen as a lack of trust in them and a move to undermine their position. Often this is not intended, so find a way or a person to call you out and remember even the very best management is not leadership.

My next point reflects how times continue to change as we enter deeper in to the twenty-first century. The importance of broadly defined ethical leadership has become, rightly, more prominent. That is not to say that an understanding of ethical behavior was ever unimportant. The very best leaders were always strong in this area, but I do see that more and more challenges are being added to the leaders' agenda, for example awareness of and strategies for environmental management, have emerged.

I place a broad definition to ethics but also one that is easy to follow. Treat all those around you—employees, teammates, senior leaders, suppliers, and customers—as you would want to be treated yourself. That is easier to write down than it is to execute on in daily life because it brings with it behaviors which can, at first, feel challenging to existing norms.

Perhaps my greatest learning in this area was when developing and delivering a turnaround strategy within a financial services business. Part of that strategy required us to cut costs aggressively, and that meant closing many operating centers and many thousands of job losses over a short time period. Historically, we would have worked hard to protect the content of plans and keep information flow to both employees and unions to a minimum.

Within the senior leadership team of the organization, there were conflicting views on how to maintain morale and operating performance in the light of such radical changes, with most leaders seeking to maintain the approach of previous years: keep the plans secret until the last possible moment. With my senior team, I concluded that an open approach with employees and unions, setting out the detail of proposals, offering a timeline of center closures and jobs losses, seeking their input on redeployment, and retraining strategies was the right way to approach the challenge. This allowed people to understand the consequences for them and enabled them to make life choices in an informed way. I tried to treat employees with trust and respect—the way I would have wanted to be treated if roles were reversed.

It worked. We sat down with the unions and explained in some detail the corporate rationale behind the need for the changes and why the changes would ensure the longer-term survival of the business and, therefore, all remaining jobs. The unions engaged closely in planning ahead for center closures and job losses. They supported training and redeployment initiatives. And whilst rightly often challenging details of the plans, not a single day was lost to industrial action and not a single meeting ever ended in deadlock.

From my perspective, your leadership ethics and morals are a part of who you are. Often, however, as a leader, only the very closest employees and colleagues will understand that. Most of the people you will lead only experience the actions and outcomes of how you lead, not the morals and ethics that drive you, unless you take steps to open up to them.

As with many large-scale companies, we undertook an annual survey of our employees' opinion on all aspects of our business. Consistent with business school teaching, we were always seeking to enhance engagement of employees as we understood how this could lead to greater and more sustainable performance, in multiple dimensions, not just financial. I was seen by many across the business, perhaps not those close to me, as a hard, performance-focused leader or, perhaps, following my earlier definition, a manager.

In the run-up to the annual survey, I took the time to share across the entire business my medium-term thoughts on how I saw the business developing, what was going well, and not so well. I sought input from colleges in open sessions on how to sustain the positive areas and what to do to address the negatives. In small and large groups, almost every employee heard the message face-to-face and was given the opportunity to raise and discuss any point they wanted to.

Most importantly, I shared my personal story—the influence of my parents, both good and challenging. The commitment and support of my wife and how our life together, and as parents, had shaped us, including the loss of two daughters and nearly a son. All had help make me the person I had become. I also shared thoughts on the leaders I have worked with that had shaped who I was. In doing this, I thought I was taking personal risk, exposing the inner workings of a forty-something mid-career leader. What actually happened was quite remarkable. An engagement from colleagues with me and a determination to drive forward the plans we had for the business that has never been surpassed in my experience.

Whilst that year employee engagement scores measured in the survey were the highest ever recorded across the company, the real success was the bond created by colleagues to the corporate goals we had set and a stronger, longer-lasting connection to me as both a leader and a person.

I had not anticipated this outcome. I had never contemplated that the openness would be so strong in creating a tie between leadership and team. People want a purpose to work for, and that is not just financial results. It is a deeper moral desire to achieve something positive, with a group of like-minded people, that can help make the world a better place for us all. Create this link and performance will be stronger and more sustainable.

What had initially convinced me to take this *risk* was a desire to treat others as I would have wanted to be treated. A selfishness on my part, to understand if others wanted to share the same vision. What I got back was an avalanche of emotion, commitment, and desire to be part of delivering that vision. Leaders need to spend as much energy engaging hearts as they do convincing minds.

I guess all this leads to another key learning. Never stop learning and developing yourself and never think you are a complete leader; there will always be more to do and more to learn. As we pass through many stages of academia, we become used to developing our technical knowledge. This applies to leadership too. There are technical aspects. The role of a business school is to help with assessing successful corporate strategies, refining business models, and sharing case studies. Leadership, however, is as much about the understanding of people, including yourself, as a leader. The life stories that sit alongside everyone's journey of change and what can be learnt only serve to help others in the future. It is the very essence of this book.

The very best leaders I have come across have been those that are always willing to learn more, always reflecting on what they have done, why they did it, and how they may have taken a different approach to improve the outcomes. They learn from good leaders they have worked with but also learn as much from bad leaders— what hasn't worked, what to avoid doing, how not to disenfranchise your colleagues. Good leaders are obsessed with self-development, but from the perspective of how to enrich what they do and for the benefit of others. Leadership is about humility and not arrogance.

That does not mean that these leaders lack confidence. In fact, it is often the opposite. There is strong confidence in shaping and delivering change and in broader aspects of success. However, this faith is not predicated solely on their own skills but a confidence in how they can bring together a motivated and skilled team. How they can shape and deliver plans together and with a knowledge that obstacles and challenges can be overcome if the team has the right basis for engaging with each other.

Seeing every opportunity to learn, always pursuing self-development, constantly self-challenging, and learning from others, good and bad, are all traits of a leader. You don't have to be the best at everything, and in fact, you will not be. A real skill of a leader is to understand not only their own strengths but also where others have expertise and real value to add and then be able to bring that capability in to the leadership group.

Being a leader is hard. It will impact your personal life and your health if you are not constantly looking at yourself and assessing and addressing any challenges or impacts being a leader is having on you. I could never have achieved my career without the support and guidance of my family and particularly my wife. They provide a great source of realism and confidence, even in the most difficult of times, and are always there to give you the feedback and counsel you sometimes need to hear to stay on top of the challenge.

Don't wait, as I did, for that darkest moment to realize that the balance between corporate life and home life has to be maintained for both to be fulfilled. Getting the balance wrong over a sustained period—committing too much time to your work life and letting it drain emotion from you—risks losing the things that are most important to you and the very reason you probably started the leadership journey.

I recall, at one stage of my career, working for a leader who was managing and undermining almost every aspect of my role. Pride and determination, usually strong features I relied upon, made me keep going and keep going in the hope that the person would evolve the way they behaved toward me. It didn't happen. I went far beyond what was sensible and, as was proved later, healthy. Eventually, after continued strong counsel from my wife, I walked away but should have learnt the lesson much more quickly. After talking to those you trust and those that care for you, don't be afraid to take a risk and leave a bad situation if you can't see a way to establish a balance.

Risk-taking is synonymous with any leadership role, both in terms of the risks of strategy and execution, but also, as we have seen, the risks to you as a leader. You should not be afraid of risk, but it does need to be regularly assessed, mitigated where possible, and acted upon when it emerges.

All change and any journey carries risk with it, regardless of how big or small. Our role as a leader is to ensure that we are aware of those risks, that warning signals are identified, and that actions are taken to mitigate as and when necessary. Although planning the journey, as we have already discussed, is a core part of leadership, risks will still emerge, and on more challenging journeys, risks that had not been identified can show up. Calmness in leading your team through these challenges, keeping stakeholders informed, and executing mitigating actions are critically important injections of confidence to your team and your stakeholders.

There are times when risks can be managed by challenging the *rules* that have been set around you. This can be really positive and lead to stretching creative thinking but must always be within the parameters of your leadership ethics, what is legal, and what is defined by regulation.

It can be an exciting time when teams start to challenge the existing field of play. New opportunities can emerge which create a step change. However, this must always be grounded in terms of the ability to make the change—speed, time, cost, skills, knowledge, etc. I always preferred answers that were aggressively evolutionary rather than revolutionary. History would seem to teach us that the ramifications of revolution are too great to me!

Regardless of any potential upside, it can never be right to break the law or break your moral code to achieve your objectives or goals. Beyond this, you must also always have an eye to the future and seek to avoid actions and decisions which, in your leadership journey, you would not be proud of in ten years' time.

So that is it. Leadership is the greatest gift that you already have embedded within you. It is also the most powerful tool you will ever have at your disposal. Use it wisely, with humility, and for the benefit of the many and not the few. Be confident in yourself, but never arrogant. Seek to learn all you can from those around you, the classroom, and those that have been on a similar journey. All you need to do is use and develop it constantly. This book will kick-start that journey and give you learnings to devour for many years to come. Good luck. I wish you well.

*T*he progress of society since the time of the early Great Lakes exploration and fur trading is familiar, but in a reflective perspective,
it was ultimately transformative.

Shipping on the Great Lakes has been an important part of the
growth of the United States and Canada since the early 1600s. The
Great Lakes are the geographical area and the natural environmental
backdrop for this incredible story. The bodies of water are a deep
blue by day and black at night. The iron ore shipping routes are
majestic, and the commerce they support is essential to economic
well-being of the entire United States of America. The daily activity
of the men and women working on the cargo freighters sailing upon
the massive bodies of fresh water provide the rich character experience throughout the book.

It seems like a very long time ago when the first European
explorers made their way into the greatest bodies of unsalted water
in the world until I reflect on my own grandparents who were born
in the 1800s. My grandparents knew American Civil War veterans
personally, and their grandparents knew Revolutionary War veterans
intimately as well. Five generations across a couple of centuries certainly connect the lives of my predecessors in a meaningful way for
me.

However, it is most certainly a long time ago when Native
Americans of the Great Lakes region, such as the Algonquins and the
Ojibwas, first interacted with the first French explorers to visit their
lands and waterways.

The earliest sailing efforts recorded on the Great Lakes were of great canoe flotillas with Native Americans bringing their fur bounty to their counterparts—the French traders. The furs came from far and wide around the Great Lakes to the annual trading fair that occurred in what is now known as Quebec during each summer. The French brought these exotic furs to the European fashion market.

It wasn't encouraged, but not forbidden, as some of the European traders moved upstream to get a jump on pelt trading at lower prices. The Europeans continued to push up steam deeper and deeper into lands surrounded by the lakes that what would become Michigan and the other Great Lake states.

In addition, there was a continuous search for a shortcut to the markets of the Far East and the Orient. The search was a constant desire to find an alternative path from the torturous voyage of sailing all the way around either the southern tip of Africa called the Cape of Good Hope or South America called Cape Horn. These endeavors drove exploration to the north and west through the Great Lakes to find a northwest crossing to speed the shipping travel time and reduce the danger of ocean transportation.

While making their imprint on the Great Lakes, all these players shaped the society that grew the frontier into the United States of America and Canada, both independent countries free from European indentureship.

Shipping continued to grow as European civilization moved into the Great Lakes region. The lakes were land locked from the east until 1825 with the opening of the Erie Cannel. There were an ever-increasing number of ships working the short shipping season of the lakes due to the frozen water of the cold weather months. People came into the area as part of a massive migration from Europe with the promise of land. As they arrived, they needed transportation and supplies. Then in turn, what the settlers grew, mined, trapped, or cut down were shipped to ports on the coast and for the growing industry in between.

Many cities developed dry docks and built ships for operation on the lakes, including the city ports from our story like Duluth, Cleveland, and Chicago. These are the impressionable ports visited by Alan and the crew of the *Demson*, making the story more vivid and seem real.

As time progressed to the Civil War of the 1860s, there were important markets for the lumber and grain of the lakes' area to feed the voracious war operations. The people of the Great Lakes provided a much-needed source of these commodities for the war effort, and the shipping transports provided the means to get these products to their proper and much desired locations.

Later came copper and iron ore mining, along with the necessary shipping in support of manufacturing and the future world wars.

As the Great Lakes matured, the shipping industry grew. The ships were made of steel and no longer wood. The hauling tonnage of the boats grew, and this one change drove down transport prices.

The number of boats increased by the time some of the characters of this fictional story come on the scene. The boats were magnificent pieces of equipment. The lake freighters were about ten times longer than wide and could haul much more than the seven thousand tons of cargo the *Demson* had capability to move. The boats could move from the end of Lake Erie to the end of Lake Superior and back in a week.

The Sault Saint Marie, or the Soo Locks, were first developed in the 1850s and were improved and deepened again and again through 1960s. The locks are destined to be improved again into the future. The Soo Locks allowed the entire Great Lakes basin to be treated as one shipping system.

This was a wonderful beginning for the people of the Midwest United States to show the world was more connected than anyone could have first conceived. Those connections continued to be expanded by the men who left and then returned to the region after fighting in two world wars. The GI Bill provided education to many of these servicemen returning from duty, which opened their opportunities to include entrepreneurism and better pay. Furthermore, the world needed the steel ore boats delivered. It provided the basic steel for the finished products the world wanted.

Social strife came to a head with the war in Vietnam. The military conflict was not well understood, and support was certainly waning by the average American as the story of Alan unfolds. Political secrecy and other social concerns, such as race relations, were being openly advocated by many on a daily basis.

By 1970, the year of this story, sports were carried on television in a more mainstream manner. Celebrity was copied and followed. A highly developed awareness of commercialism by the average American family was on the rise. Credit cards and easy credit made their way into more and more households, and the practice of revolving credit began to be accepted as a norm within our way of living.

This is a work of fiction, but it contains a realistic backdrop of the times. The story touches on the Vietnam War, the Nixon-era politics, an active media, the further demise of Detroit, race awareness, and big business sway into their employees' lives and values. The activities on an ore boat working on the Great Lakes in the summer of 1970 are very much weaved into this story.

The progress of society since the time of the early Great Lakes exploration and fur trading is familiar but in a reflective perspective it was ultimately transformative. The United States of America became a country, the Civil War tore apart the North and South regions of the country, internal conflicts occurred in the Great Lakes area, including business strategy, border defense, and statesmanship, and of course, the two revealing world wars were unraveled which were fought and supported overwhelmingly by the men and women of the Great Lakes' states and Michigan in particular. Best of all, the Industrial Revolution arrived with manufacturing and modern invention while bringing succeeding generations the automobile, the telephone, the electric everything, and then, of course, the computer. The computer age was in its beginning stages as the story of Alan's summer in 1970 was unfolding.

With this is mind, I have been writing this book for almost fifty years. Most of that time, it has been in my head. I grew up in Wadhams, five miles west of Port Huron. I have recounted the events of my summer of 1970 many times. The adventure was between my freshman and sophomore years in college. Because I graduated from high school at seventeen, I couldn't get a job that was industrial in nature until one year later when I was eighteen, during that fateful summer of 1970.

These were exciting times for a naive young man from a small town in Michigan. It allowed him to grow up, but also remain optimistic and fresh. It also provided a platform for good leader behavior and moral fiber. The principles in the book were not always evident to me. It took a career and a lifetime to distill these principles into a cogent argument for their effectiveness.

Until recently, I had been working as a senior executive at a large utility. I now have the desire and time to write this book. It is fiction work with a realistic tone that should make it both believable, entertaining, and maybe a bit more exciting.

I have a wonderful wife, Christine, of forty-five years who, with me, raised our two children, Nicole and Andrew.

Christine is an accomplished educator. She graduated from the University of Michigan with a mathematics degree and a political science minor. She moved with me as I was able to go from construction job to construction job and progressed through a consulting start-up and into the utility business. She rode each of these waves with style and zest.

With her degree, she educated young people, especially young women, to be very good in mathematics, including calculus, geometry, and algebra. But she urged them to reach for even more advancement in the sciences and computer programming. She caused her students to be better people. She worked in four distinct school districts with different demographics and cultures. She often pressed for curriculum changes and finally drove robotic endeavors into the classroom.

All the while, she was home with our children when they needed it, ensured they were safe and experienced in matters of the world. She helped coach the problem solving and science clubs in which they participated. She always encouraged and comforted me and our family. Our children were accomplished students with advanced degrees. Indeed, they are accomplished citizens of the world.

We are all well traveled and have seen much of the world from the Caribbean, Mexico, Central America, Europe, Asia, and the entire

United States. We have met many rich and powerful people. But we have chosen to live as we did long ago. We are average Americans. We are self-described as wholesome and honest people.

Our children are grown and have children of their own. They are accomplished one and all. It is fun to see them progress in their lives and their hopes for our grandchildren.

This book is especially for my family. I hope my grandchildren can find in the story for an opening into the history of family with insight from five generations of grandparents, parents, and children. The reader will discover a bit of me and my experience in the pages of this work. They can also find the leadership principles I profess. I also hope they can take to heart the story of Alan and, ultimately, allow honesty and truth to win the day.

The leadership lessons are imbedded in the storytelling to facilitate the context of the events and allow the outcomes of the action to be internalized and digested. The truths and fiction of the story are supplied for the reader to contemplate and to maybe cause each one to wonder about their own future.

I have written this book to help me to never forget how my values and character have shaped how I managed my past. I truly appreciate those people I have studied and worked with over the years. I know these men and women have influenced me to be a more mature and caring man.

Finally, I want to open a dialogue as to the nature of our lives. We can make a difference. Pick the appropriate purpose for your life and move toward it. We are all leaders in the roles we fulfill. It is not the hierarchy of an organization that describes who is a leader, but it is the nature and character of the people themselves and how they behave. Everyone leads at some time in the course of their daily activities.

I love you, Lucas George Dunham, Jacob Ron Dunham, Ryleigh Alexis May, and Cameron David May.

I love you, Nicole Kristen Lambert May and Andrew Ryan May and his wife, Torrie L. May.

I love you, Christine Denise Lambert May. You are my standard to judge how I am doing, and you are my love.

CHAPTER 1

· · · · · · · · ● ● ● ● ● ● ● · · · · ·

A CALL WAS MADE

"How did this happen without me knowing?" asked Alan.

Elm yelled, "Alan, come here!" Alan didn't know what she wanted, but his mother doesn't yell with that tone very often. She sounded excited but with a bit of an anxious tone.

Alan was lying on his full bed, listening to an eight-track player.

Of course, bigger was better, and therefore, the eight-track player seemed desirable over the smaller beta compact cassette player in 1970. Eight-track players were first invented and then offered in Learjets and later in automobiles. It provides music on an endless loop of lubricated tape which is not good for long-term quality. The cassette player didn't employ either of these attributes and would win out over the longer haul.

Alan had the volume up, maybe too loud, and was singing along, "When you're weary, feeling small. When tears are in your eyes, I'll dry them all. I'm on your side, oh, when times get tough, and friends just can't be found. Like a bridge over troubled water. I will lay me down." This is Simon and Garfunkel's best song in Alan's opinion.

Alan is eighteen. He graduated from high school at seventeen and couldn't get a job working in industry until he turned eighteen, which is now about six months ago. This summer would be his first opportunity to work at an industrial job, making union wages. His college classes were at a local junior college and were finished a week earlier with excellent results. He was invited to join Phi Beta Kappa.

Alan is tall like his mother's father, Cap'n, who was six foot tall. Alan at six feet, two inches is thin but muscular. He has moderately long, dark hair, and brown eyes. His boyish face makes him look a bit younger than he is. Because he graduated from high school a year ago and has been attending college and studying engineering, he still lives at home. Therefore, Alan lives with his mother and father and along with his two siblings in a small village outside Port Huron, Michigan. This has been his only home since birth.

Alan thought he had heard his mother's voice and turned the music down. He yelled from his room, "Did you call? I'll be right there!"

His bedroom was on the second floor of the small framed cottage. He went out of his room and along a short hall. He bounded down the enclosed staircase and went around a corner and into the largest room in the house, the kitchen. "What is it?" Allen asked. "What do you want?"

Elm was at the oblong walnut-stained wooden table, looking at the mail. She worked part-time but was home almost every day when her *kids* were out of school. She is tall for a woman of her time and has dark hair with blue eyes. She is beaming.

"Your uncle, Rap, has arranged a position for you on an ore boat. You can work for the Steel Company just like Uncle Rap and your grandfather, Cap'n, did. However, this is only a summer job and you have to return to your engineering studies in the fall. You will have a few days to get ready. You know, I am so excited for you." She stood up and gave him a hug.

Rap is Elm's brother-in-law, her sister's Amp's husband. Rap worked as a captain on the Great Lakes for many years and had recently retired after a harrowing escape from disaster on Lake Superior.

Elm had told Alan the story of Rap's terrifying experience almost two years earlier. Rap confided in Elm that it was the worst near-death encounter he experienced in his thirty-five years of sailing on the lakes.

Elm told the story, and it was terrifying. "It was mid-November. The boat, over six hundred feet long, became crosswise with the waves rolling across the lake. This is not usual, but it can happen at points in the lake where the land and the wind move the waves in different directions. Rap's vessel listed about forty degrees. The load didn't shift, or the boat would have kept on rolling over. With quick wheelsman action, the boat was turned out of the trough with only one of its two propellers still in the water. The other screw was lifted out of the churning water because of the tilt of the boat and the rolling waves receding away from the vessel. The boat was righted, but it left the crew totally spooked. They were in a near-disastrous incident and their faces showed it. Rap and his crew were quite lucky, and they very well could have been on the bottom of the lake. Rap left the life he knew so well and for so long. He retired the next month, in December, at the end of the season."

Elm flatly stated, "There has been talk about drinking on board that night. Nothing came of the rumors as everyone was safe after the ordeal. But Rap decided to retire at the end of the season, about a month later after an investigation. It took a lot out of Rap."

Elm continued in a lecturing manner, "Alan, beware. Even your worst actions should be available for television on the eleven o'clock news."

Now Alan is being told that he was going to be working on one of the Steel Company's burned-red behemoth boats. He was caught off guard. Alan thought to himself, he had a job opportunity on a lake freighter? What actions did he need to take?

"How did this happen without me knowing?" asked Alan.

Elm apologized and said, "Everyone knows this simple principle. It is hard for people when change occurs to them and they are not in the loop. We know people want to be in the conversation when decisions are made that will change their lives. Hard as it seems when things aren't certain, people want to know what is changing and how it will affect them. This principle wasn't applied in this case, Alan."

Elm continued, "Well, we didn't want to tell you about the job until it was assured. Uncle Rap's first mate, named Brads, has been promoted and will be the captain on your boat, the *C. M. Demson*. You will be a deckhand or a wiper, depending on what they need when you report of duty on Sunday."

"Wow, this Sunday! So soon!" Alan exclaimed woefully.

Alan breathed hard and then asked, "Does Dad know?"

"Yup," Elm said. "I called him just before I called you down."

Alan couldn't believe what was happening. His plans for the summer include friends, his family, working at some job, and maybe some camping.

He thought he could work at a local store again for the summer or maybe get a job in a local factory. At the store, he knew could barely earn minimum wage. Although in a store he wouldn't make enough money for next year's tuition at college, but it would be easier to get hired.

In a factory, he could get a union wage plus overtime pay if offered. But he hadn't even applied for a single better-paying position a week after finals were concluded. Was it fear or lack of knowledge that kept him from pursuing the necessary higher wage-earning job?

Given all this, the inability to earn enough for school was wearing on Alan. He even thought he might have to skip a semester or two along the way to make ends meet. It was a complete bust and not a good plan.

However, this was a real chance to get ahead of his education bills, but he had to leave home.

"Dag nab it!" Alan said under his breath. He learned the cuss phrase from his dad who learned it from his dad, Alan's grandfather. Leaving home was an inevitable outcome, but it came at him in a rush!

Alan needed to be flexible. This is a principle that he could carry with him and apply throughout the rest of his life. Alan said to himself, "Be open to an alternative path, and when the opportunity comes to better yourself, take it."

Alan was thoughtful in the moment, and the trade-offs seemed well worth the abrupt change that was impending. Of course, he had no choice and decided to take the opportunity without a fight.

"Okay." Alan was all in, and the beaming smile on his face showed it. Remember, there was no other answer that would have been acceptable.

Alan concluded that there is almost always a yes to any question asked or opportunity presented, but many times there must be a modification in some way to achieve it. This time, Alan wanted to negotiate for more time, but he also knew it was a settled argument. Either take the job on Sunday or miss the chance to earn enough for school in the fall and ultimately disappoint everyone, even himself.

A few minutes later, Ham, Alan's dad, drove into the driveway. He had a beige four-door 1966 Bel Air Chevrolet. Elm and Alan went out to meet him. Ham turned off the car, and the engine knocked a bit before finally being silent. Ham said under his breath, "The engine is still sucking air and a bit of fuel through the carburetor and into a couple of cylinders. It will need a tune-up soon."

He stepped out of the car. He was slight, but strong. He gave his son a heartfelt hug.

Ham started, "I talked to Rap. Tomorrow we are going to drive to Detroit and go to the Federal Building to get a Merchant Mariner's Document for you. The Steel Company will have made them aware that you have a position, and all you need is your birth certificate and a photo. Uncle Rap suggested that you use one of your high school pictures. I know it is a bit formal and you look different now with longer hair, but it will do. You will be listed as a deckhand and a wiper. Uncle Rap will go with us."

Alan asked almost immediately after Ham was finished, "What's a wiper?"

Ham said, "I don't know, but we can ask Rap tomorrow. I am certain it is not what you think it is!" They all smiled.

The three began talking about the next day, the next week and imagining Alan's job on into the summer. They went into their modest home and had dinner with Alan's sister and brother, Carol and Bert. Everyone was excited but nervous about what was to come. The family had never really been apart over Alan's entire lifetime. All that was about to change.

Dinner consisted of toasted white bread and peas and chicken gravy to pour over the toast. The chicken came from the farm of Elm's parents. Alan's grandmother raised chickens to sell for frying and for the eggs. She raised fruit and vegetables, along with a few rabbits.

Desert that night was a bowl of apple sauce that Elm had made the previous fall. It was good and filling. Tellingly, Alan drank a half gallon of milk at the meal. He was a big eater, and he cost Ham and Elm a lot for groceries.

Carol and Alan did the dishes in the kitchen sink. Carol is the washer, and Alan the dryer. Occasionally, there was a little something left on a plate or spoon, and Alan would point it out to Carol. She would simply respond, "A good dryer should catch it and wipe it away."

After dinner was done, the talk subsided, and Alan went up to his room. He noticed things like the sounds of the freight trucks pushing past his home. Their lights would move over the ceiling as they rounded the curve in the road near the front of the house. He lived on a main road between parts suppliers and auto factories, and the long-distant haulers used the road running past Alan's house as their main route.

In addition, he heard the woeful sound of the railroad engines pulling their railcars while coming upon a road crossing. This stretch of railroad connected the two countries of the United States of America and Canada. It was a busy track, but timetables governed when the trains would pass nearby Alan's home. It was nearing ten at night.

Alan couldn't sleep that night and wondered what the next few days would bring.

CHAPTER 2

· · · · · · · ● ● ● ● ● ● ● ● · · ·

MAKING READY

Alan hugged him and said, "Thank you."

The next morning, the three men drove to Detroit. Rap generally drove everywhere he went. It was a bit of a control method for him. But Rap decided to ride with Alan and Ham in their family's big sedan, the '66 Chevy. Alan was in the back seat. They packed sandwiches and coffee for the older men on the trip. Alan had a local favorite Faygo Rock & Rye pop to drink.

It was overcast and gray. The temperature was in the fifties when they left Port Huron. There was no rain in the forecast, but the wind was gusty.

Almost immediately after picking up Uncle Rap, Alan asked, "What's a wiper?"

Rap laughed. "A wiper is an aft crew member that gets to do anything anyone else doesn't want to do. Essentially, there are three wipers on board an ore boat, one per shift. They wipe up grease and oil and are an all-around helper. Sometimes they're called a gopher. Go for this and go for that."

Rap went on, "There are three shifts on a lake freighter, and generally, you will find three of most positions. There are three wipers, three oilers, three licensed engineers, and the singular chief engineer. There are three deckhands, a boatswain mate, three watchmen, three wheelsmen, three mates, and a singular captain. There is a chief cook, an assistant cook, and two stewards."

Alan took a deep breath and thought about what he heard. "I guess I am glad I could have a chance to work both ends of the boat, both a deckhand and a wiper. On the other hand, it seems like the crew would be a bit divided by the type of work they do. However, it also seems like the galley could be a common location for all crew members to meet and talk, just like the kitchen seems to be the place a family spends a lot of their time together."

Rap said, "The officers will eat together in the dining room. The off-shift people will eat as they can during the night. There is always food available in the large stainless steel coolers to grab and eat. But the day crews will certainly find more overlapping times to eat, talk, and tell tales in the galley."

Rap went on to say, "I would really like you to be a deckhand. I told Brads this. That way, you will be in the middle of the vessel operations at all times and with access to the wheelhouse when asked. The officers are nearby, and you can observe them when they're on duty. You will learn a lot about character and decision-making."

Ham added, "Don't expect a close-knit crew, especially at first. The men are working to make a living and come from a variety of different backgrounds. You will have to work to fit in."

The traffic was getting congested as they continued to drive through the close-in suburbs of Detroit, like Roseville, East Detroit, and Grosse Pointe. The freeway on which they rode began construction in 1956 during the Eisenhower administration. The transportation system idea was to find a quick way to move defense vehicles around the country. Of course, it also provided a safe and faster way to move commercial trucks and private cars on a daily basis. For the past fourteen years, the highway system had been under construction and it appeared to Alan as though it will continue for another twenty years and maybe more.

Then Rap changed the subject. "Ever been arrested, Alan?" Alan looked shocked. "If you had, the Federal Bureau of Investigation will check you out and deny your documentation."

Rap knew Alan was going to be cleared by the background check but wanted to put Alan on notice to be on his best behavior when he took the ore boat summer job. Rap had recommended Alan to his friend, Captain Brads. It would be a good thing for Alan to be a good worker and have a stellar character while working on the *C. M. Demson*.

"Of course not," Alan laughed. "I have never even gotten a traffic ticket."

However, Alan knew of a couple of his high school classmates who had been arrested for auto theft and drug possession, respectively. He was never part of any of their criminal activities. Alan thought, what a step backward if anyone would start out the beginning their adult life with a criminal record. It would be impossible to get a job like the opportunity Alan has been given.

"Don't break the law," Alan repeated to himself. This seems like a very simple rule to remember and keep. Why are there so many people who can't control themselves? Is it greed, rage, revenge, power, or is there something else buried in their basic makeup?

Alan thought that he could always come from a point of view that everyone is well-meaning unless they are proven otherwise. He would treat everyone with respect, and by doing so, he would be giving himself the best chance to have more friends and better outcomes and to have a more successful and happy life.

Alan vowed that power, money, and position would not always be the foremost factors in his endeavors, but he would try to always try applying compassion, goodness, and kindness. He also promised that he would try to lead a healthy lifestyle. He would eat well, exercise, and practice safe behaviors. These would be the cornerstones of his life.

Alan said to Rap and his father flatly, "No, I haven't been arrested, and I will live my life in a way that I never put myself in that position."

When they arrived in Detroit, Ham steered the car off the freeway and onto a wide city street. Alan was a bit nervous. Three years earlier, the city of Detroit had one of the worst race riots of the 1960s. The year 1967 experienced sixteen riots across America, five of them were in Michigan and nearby Toledo, Ohio. Then Detroit had another smaller riot in 1968 after Martin Luther King was shot in Memphis, Tennessee.

Now the common thought in other parts of the State of Michigan and elsewhere was that much of the "city of Detroit was burned down." The black residents of Detroit were dangerous and violent and that white visitors were unwelcomed. This was a troubling belief for Alan. He heard Motown songs that were created not far from where he was going. He knew about auto factories in Detroit. He tried to remember that he wanted to come from a point of view that everyone is well-meaning unless they are proven otherwise.

After several turns and reverses, they finally found the Federal Building. Ham found a manned parking lot nearby. He parked the car and paid the white attendant five dollars.

The building was large and seemed to take a large portion of a whole city block. They went inside, asked directions from a receptionist, passed through a light security checkpoint, and went up an elevator to the third floor.

When they got off the elevator, the three men moved directly up to the counter. The process was surprisingly easy. Alan's fingerprints were taken, his birth certificate copied and recorded, and his high school picture was verified as Alan.

The Merchant Mariner's Document card was prepared and compared to the information provided by the Steel Company. In the end, the laminated documentation card, with Alan's picture embossed, was produced, and it was slightly larger than a driver's license.

The nominal cost of the licensing fee was paid by Ham in cash, and then the three went down the elevator and out the door. They didn't say a word.

They briskly walked across the street and down the block to the parking lot where the car was parked. When the three men arrived at the lot, the parking attendant wasn't anywhere to be found. The car was fine, but Ham apparently paid a scam artist to park in a vacant lot. Ham said, "Dag nab it." They got in the car and were happy to be on their way.

The ride home was filled with country music and small talk. Merle Haggard was singing, "But when they're runnin' down our country, man, they're walkin' on the fightin' side of me."

On the way home, Alan asked Rap, "What are the working hours and the pay on board the boat?"

Rap replied, "You work anytime you're in port if you're a deckhand. You will be compensated with time off the next day if it exceeds eight hours. You don't work on Sunday. You get paid for forty hours a week, and you should take your entire pay at the end of the summer. You don't have anything to spend it on anyway. Lastly, you get room and board. You know, they give you food to eat, and they don't charge you."

When the men returned home, they dropped off Rap. Alan hugged him and said, "Thank you."

Rap said, "My pleasure. Remember, this is not a career move. Stay with your engineering education and come home safe." Alan wouldn't see Rap again until his adventure was nearly completed. Amp waved from her front door.

Elm greeted the travelers as they entered their home. "I am glad you're here. Alan, tomorrow you need to visit your grandfather," she said mournfully. "I am not sure he will make it through the summer. This could be your last chance to see him."

"Your start date is just a couple of days away," stated Ham. "Get some sleep and then let's begin to pack for your adventure ahead."

CHAPTER 3

UP AND UNDERSTANDING

It is meticulous work and sometimes difficult
with equipment change outs and inspections
in the bitterly cold weather of February.

Alan woke up. It was a few minutes after seven. He was in his bed. As he lay there, he thought for a moment that maybe he had been just dreaming about leaving his tiny village just outside Port Huron called Wadhams. He softly sang a little song he made up about the four-corner stop on the highway. Then he spotted the Merchant Mariner's Document on his nightstand.

Reality struck! He realized that the job away from home was true. He was going away and the events over the next few months would change him forever.

Coincidently, Port Huron was the boyhood home of Thomas Edison. Tom moved to Port Huron when he was seven with his family in 1854, not quite one hundred years before Alan was born.

This is the city that formed Edison's understanding of literature, business, farming, and how to work very long and productive days. When Edison was in his early teens, he sold his mother's vegetable produce and developed a market for his newspapers using the telegraph. The telegraph provided the news, and Edison put that news on paper.

He produced newspapers on the train from Port Huron to Detroit and back. His business grew as the Civil War ensued, and the traffic on the trains grew immensely. The news the train-riding population wanted, Edison was able to provide. This is also the time when Edison started a fire on the train while testing one of his chemistry experiments, and the conductor put him off at Smith's Creek, damaging Edison's eardrums. Smith's Creek is not far from Alan's home.

Edison's accomplishments included inventing the light bulb and a phonograph for which he recorded "Mary Had a Little Lamb."

Although Port Huron's common claim to fame is Thomas Edison, there is much more to the town than that of a connection with one of the influential American men who moved society to a more modern existence. Its geography is a key to its history. Port Huron sits at the base of Lake Huron, one of the five Great Lakes in the Midwestern United States. The southern peninsula of Michigan looks like a mitten. Port Huron is in Southeast Michigan, just south of the area called the Thumb. It is located directly across from Canada, connected by a bridge of six thousand feet.

The military, lumber, farming, and transportation, in one form or another, have been part of the way of life in Port Huron since discovered by French Europeans led by an explorer called du Lhut in 1686.

Duluth, Minnesota, is named after this explorer and will become a place Alan will know well and remember. It is a place the ore boats port to take on iron ore from the mines of Minnesota and beyond.

The real community establishment began in 1814 after the War of 1812 with a permanent garrison near the present-day town of Port Huron called Fort Gratiot. With the war concluded and safety enhanced, settlement roots were in place to allow commerce to grow and families to arrive.

Alan's family came to Port Huron in the mid-1800s, just like Edison's family. They were coopers, farmers, barn builders, teachers, and hotel operators. Alan's grandfathers either worked for the railroad or shipping on the Great Lakes.

With its proximity to the shipping passages of the Great Lakes, many seamen have lived in Port Huron and the nearby towns and villages up and down the St. Clair River, connecting Lake Huron with Lake St. Clair and onto Detroit. The shipping lanes provide access to ships from all over the world as they pass by the Port Huron. Residents wave at the boats and their crew, and the wheelsmen and officers on the vessels blow their high decibel steam-driven horns in return with one prolonged blast followed by two short ones. This is especially true of the boats that carry iron ore from the northern Midwest mines to the hungry steel mills in Michigan, Pennsylvania, and Ohio.

The sailors on the ore boats wish their families goodbye in February as they leave home to fit out their assigned vessels. This effort includes starting up all the systems and making sure that they are fit for use. It is meticulous work and sometimes difficult with equipment change outs and inspections in the bitterly cold weather of February.

The crew designations are interesting. The captains, of course, are assigned to their boat by their preference through seniority. The newest, largest boats usually get selected first. The only variance from this practice would be an act of superstition. A boat that had difficulty, such as death of a crew member or an unfortunate sailing incident, could be opted out by the captain. His choice would be to take another vessel and leave the decision on the *afflicted* boat to the next officer.

The rest of the crew members are assigned, with officers and senior sailors making their boat choices known first. A captain could deny a crew member's choice if the captain was aware of an issue and didn't like their capabilities or how they would fit into the crew makeup. Then the remaining crew members were chosen and hired.

The crew needed to have their boats ready when the Sault Ste. Marie or Soo Locks were opened after the ice of the winter dissipated usually in early March. As the season progressed, personnel changed and new crew members were added. Alan would be one of these adds, not dissimilar to other company bosses and their college-aged sons.

These men work through the tough spring weather, endure the storms and heat of the summer, and finally fight their way through the fall gales and early winter cold and misery. The seamen finally make it home for Christmas.

This life is hard on the men and their families. How does a sailor integrate his life with work on the lakes and the family needs?

The wife of the sailor is usually very strong-willed, has great spirit, and can handle most situations alone. She raises their children and manages the household and the family finances. Telephone calls are made a couple of times per week, a letter is occasionally sent, and the rare sighting at the water's edge is the most she can hope for.

The sailor is bound to a routine, a schedule, and the hope of connection as the world passes by. This is tortuous if trust is not the basis for his family relationships. If the family is intact after a few seasons, the career as a sailor and sailor's wife is probably fitting for everyone involved. Alan knew of this life as the life of his grandparents and aunt and uncle.

The crew members fight their way through the fear of the night water on the lakes. When it is dark and the boat is out of sight of land, there is no light from anywhere but your own decks. Sometimes the sky can be gray and overcast. With these conditions, the moon and the stars are not easily seen and the water is black.

However, the fear of the blackness of the lakes at night can be overcome. Here is a Thomas Edison story he told that sheds some light on the process of overcoming fear:

Edison sold newspapers in Port Huron where he arrived by the daily train from Detroit about nine thirty at night. He didn't arrive home until eleven thirty. On the way home from the train station, he passed by a thicket near the road where about three hundred soldiers were buried. They died of the disease called cholera a long time prior to Edison's arrival. However, it was disturbing to the young man, and he would shut his eyes and push the horse to gallop past the graveyard. On occasion, the horse would step on something that would snap. This would give Edison a jolt and a heartfelt jump. As is the way of people, after many rides, the trip became tiresome and all concern about the travel past the dead totally disappeared.

In other words, if nothing happens when you are in the middle of a terrifying activity, your mind begins to believe that nothing will ever happen. This is particularly interesting for those men who have had friends and family members who have met a tragic death in the Great Lakes. They still sail the lakes without fear.

This phenomenon is called behavioral exposure. The more you are exposed to what scares you, the more effective it becomes in conditioning you not to be afraid. It doesn't mean the activity isn't dangerous or could actually hurt you. It just means you aren't afraid of it!

CHAPTER 4

· · · · · · · · · ● ● ● · · · · · · · ·

MORE TO DO

Alan thought about what this adventure meant to him.

Alan began to think about what to pack for the summer. He said to himself, "I need work boots." These he would buy himself on the way back from seeing Cap'n, and almost all the rest of his gear would be things he already owned. He didn't want to place any additional burden on his parents although a duffel bag was being contributed by Rap, which he used over the years to transport his laundry.

Alan went downstairs and had a breakfast of two bowls of cold cereal called Raisin Bran, produced by Kellogg's a Michigan company headquartered in Battle Creek. He listened to the radio which was tuned to a Detroit news station, WJR. The reports had commercials from Hudson's, a local Detroit department store, about reupholstering of a sofa. There was a car commercial providing all the features of the Chevrolet Camaro and a Sears and Roebuck's work clothing sale advertisement.

The news headline was that President Nixon was looking for a compromise with the Senate on a Vietnam War Bill. "In other news," the announcer droned on. The United Auto Workers Union was closing the field of candidates to head the behemoth international union headquartered in Detroit. The price-wage lid was scrapped because it wasn't believed by Nixon that it would hold inflation in check. Finally, layoffs loomed in a city neighboring Detroit due to a cash crunch.

Detroit Mayor Gribbs attended a baseball game between the eventual major-league baseball East Division champions, Baltimore Orioles and the Detroit Tigers, at Tiger Stadium. The very average Tigers won four to nothing in a blowout in that game. Earl Weaver and rookie sensation, Thurman Munson, were quoted for Baltimore. Tiger greats Willie Horton, Al Kaline, and Jim Northrup were reported as standouts in the game's scoring.

Alan wasn't very interested in the news generally, but he had become more aware of the politics that moved him closer toward being drafted by the United States Army. He was a full-time student, but he was aware if he wasn't, he could easily be drafted as had many of his high school friends. He enjoyed sports, especially baseball, and was happy to hear the sporting news. The Tigers had won the World Series in 1968. Many of the same players are still on the team. Mayo Smith is still the manager. They seem to be tired and spent and simply have no spark this year.

However, on this day, Alan was more interested in the background noises he found familiar. He enjoyed the creaks of the kitchen floor from family members making their way through their daily routines, the hum of cars and trucks on the road in the front of the house, and birds' songs outside in the trees. He was going to miss all this.

He went out for a walk in the yard. It is spring and a cooler day than normal. The yard is large, and it covers four acres, including a stand of deciduous trees, which were full of brilliant green leaves. Alan smiled as he thought about not mowing the yard this summer for the first time in many years. The walk was a nice break before he went to see Cap'n, his grandfather. Alan thought about what this adventure meant to him.

It wasn't lost on Alan that he had been given a great opportunity because he was a relative of a captain. They call it nepotism, and it is an appropriate word. Per the dictionary, it is "the practice among those with power or influence of favoring relatives or friends, especially by giving them jobs." The definition fit him perfectly.

Alan determined that he would be worthy of the position by working hard and have exemplary character. However, it was still his relative getting him the job. Alan thought that this was how those in power pass along opportunities to their next generation. Alan's résumé would forever show this important summer job. He would be thought of differently by friends and prospective employers. He would have a unique skill set that would be transportable to other positions, especially in the industrialized world.

The perplexed smile crossed his face. It was getting late and he needed to go.

CHAPTER 5

· · · · · · · ● · ● · · · · · · · ·

GOING TO VISIT CAP'N

At night, the water turns a black blue.

"Hey, Jude, don't make it bad. Take a sad song and make it better. Remember to let her into your heart. Then you can start to make it better." Alan is singing along with the Beatles on the radio, and he is quite tone worthy.

The song is fitting. It was his favorite Beatles song from his senior year in high school in 1968 and through graduation in the summer of 1969. It is also appropriate as he is going to visit his grandfather on his deathbed. Both sad but with a good reminder that things can get better as time passes.

Finishing high school was a culmination of thirteen years of growth. Growing from age four to age seventeen certainly puts a sharp focus on the rest of your life. Being fair, honest, and giving more than you take will surely be tested by circumstances over time.

Nonetheless, making it to that graduation achievement was wonderful and a bit melancholy. Youth and childhood are left behind, and as time passes, people you love die.

You can make it better by remembering fondly what it has taken to get to the present, and without promises, you can dream about the future.

At eighteen, Alan is driving his black 1962 Studebaker station wagon with red interior which he acquired by way of his parents from his grandfather, Cap'n. The car is a Lark. There is a joke lurking in these words. Alan loves "play on word" jokes or puns. The car is not a popular brand, and in fact, the Studebaker went out of business four years earlier in 1966. The car reflects Alan's demeanor. He isn't all that popular but is steady and hardworking.

The radio is dialed into the CKLW the AM rock station from Windsor, Ontario, Canada, and volume is way up. The front windows are down and on this late-May day. The weather in southeast Michigan is cool but sunny.

Alan is on his way to the county hospital for long-term care. His grandfather is in the facility due to complications from type 2 diabetes.

His grandfather had recently been on a Great Lakes pleasure cruise a few months earlier. The cruise began at Montreal, Quebec, Canada. The ship came upstream by way of the Saint Lawrence Seaway through the Welland Canal locks around the Niagara Falls. The cruise proceeded across Lake Erie, up the Detroit River, across Lake St. Clair, and into Lake Huron. Then they made their way through the waters of Lake Huron to the Soo Locks, into Lake Superior, and onto Duluth, Minnesota. On the return trip, they traced the path back to the Soo, then down under the Mighty Mackinaw Span linking the two peninsulas of Michigan, and finally south through Lake Michigan to Chicago. The cruise took ten days and was a great reminder of the sailing trips the former captain traveled so many times throughout his life.

The Great Lakes are beautiful to look at from the land or the water. The water is a deep blue by day, and the white caps of the waves are spectacular to see. The white seagulls follow the boats to get scraps to eat from the galley waste.

The night is full of stars, and if you find yourself in Lake Superior, the Northern Lights might be seen. At night, the water turns a blue black and you can swear you see waterborne monsters lurking next to the vessel that follow the slip of water down the hull or out into the waves extending from the bow of the boat.

The food is fantastic on a cruise, and the nightly conversations with a veteran sailor is a hit.

This was the vacation the old captain wanted and thoroughly enjoyed.

The cruise liner was smaller than the thousand footer Cap'n last commanded. With its size, the waves of the lakes were felt as the short chop was constantly pushing at the boat's sides. As the weather changed, there were small squalls at times.

One morning, the boat lurched as the waves were whipped by the wind. The old captain slipped and scraped his left leg on a grated steel tread on a stairway while going up to the galley from his stateroom for breakfast.

The scrape became quite infected after a few weeks with Cap'n performing his self-medicating care, a practice which he had administered his whole life. The salve he used was not strong enough to stop the internal infection now in his bloodstream. Over time, as the wound became infected, gregarine spread throughout his leg. He should have gone to a doctor sooner.

When he did go to the doctor, it was too late. To try to save the old man's life, the leg was amputated. Even with this drastic procedure, the infection invaded his entire body, and the expectation was he would die over the summer of 1970. He was seventy-seven. Visiting Cap'n at the urging of his mother, Alan knew this visit could very well be the last time he would see his grandfather alive.

CHAPTER 6

THE VISIT'S TWIST

Alan said, "Thank you, but I am here to see Cap'n."

Alan is excited to visit his grandfather because he is about to begin an adventure of his lifetime. With Alan being accepted as a deckhand, he will continue a family legacy. He is deckhand on the *C. M. Demson*, an iron ore-carrying freighter built in 1918. It is owned and operated by the Steel Company and has a special history with Cap'n. The *Demson* was clearly one of the oldest boats in the fleet at fifty-two years. She had been built in response to steel needs of the First World War. To Alan, it had a great ring of appeal. To Cap'n, it was one of his first commands as captain.

Cap'n was the fleet captain for the Steel Company and had retired a little over ten years earlier. The fleet captain could have his pick of any boat in the fleet based upon his seniority. He had chosen one of the new one-thousand-foot behemoths and clearly hadn't sailed on the *Demson* for some time. Alan had seen a picture of his mother, Elm, with her dad, Cap'n, on the *Demson* when she looked about fourteen. That was a quite a while ago, over twenty years.

Cap'n began his sailing career on a similar long freighter in 1907, and he also started as a deckhand. Cap'n was just fifteen. He was larger than other boys his age, and he was strong. He lied about his age.

Alan parked his car and was a bit reluctant to emerge from the vehicle due to the gravity of the visit. As he turned off his car, Santana was singing, "Black magic woman. Got a black magic woman. I got a black magic woman. Got me so blind, I can't see."

With Alan being aware that this could possibly be his final visit with his grandfather, he wanted it to be a memorable one. Alan gathered his thoughts and exited the car. He stretched his six feet, two inches frame. He had dark hair over his ears in Beatles style and had a wiry, hardened frame. His stride was confident, and he limberly gained the steps to the half floor above the ground and entered the building.

Alan asked the attendant at the front desk, "Which room is Cap'n's? He's my grandfather."

Alan had not been in this hospital before. In fact, he was only in a hospital three times in his life: when he was born at over ten pounds, when he had his tonsils out, and the third time in high school when he had pneumonia so severe that he was dehydrated, virally weakened, and needed intensive care.

This hospital made him nervous. It felt a little like a patient had to be in a hopeless state to be admitted. This was not a place for healing but simply existing.

The attendant gave Alan the room number and the general direction. It was obvious the best staff were not employed in this facility. They were lackluster and a bit rude. It seemed like Alan had asked for a great imposition when he simply wanted to know where his grandfather's room was.

Alan made it down the hall, and the numbers to the rooms were stenciled on the doors. When the doors were open, the room numbers couldn't be seen easily without partially entering the room.

Alan looked for the number on the door down the hall when he thought was close to Cap'n's room. He had to partially enter the room as he read the number on the door. Immediately, there stood a nurse next to a long-term patient in a white linen-draped hospital bed. It was ghostlike.

Alan felt he was violating a space that was very personal. He was embarrassed and wanted to duck out.

In the crisp bed lay a young man Alan thought was around his age. Alan said sheepishly, "Hi. I am Alan. I am so sorry for interrupting you."

The young man was drawn and very thin. He had no visible muscle mass. It looked like he had been in the bed a very long time.

The young man said very softly, "No problem. I am Charlie."

The nurse said, "Charlie has been here since he was about eight. He was in a terrible swimming accident. He dove from a bridge about five miles from here."

Upon reflection for a moment, Alan knew the young frail man. He had been a classmate of Alan's. Charlie dove from a nearby bridge into shallow water the summer before he was going into third grade. He had broken his neck. He was completely paralyzed from his neck to his toes.

It was an awful thing when their third-grade teacher explained what happened later in September. Of course, Alan knew of the accident but didn't know until that moment that Charlie was still alive and at this facility.

Charlie was painting with a small brush in his mouth. Alan could see his work all over the walls. The art was good, but all the paintings were of water scenes, including one of a shipwreck. The water was dark, and the waves were splashing high into the air over the bow of the ship.

The nurse said to Alan, "Come into Charlie's room for a visit."

Alan said, "Thank you, but I am here to see Cap'n."

The nurse said with dejection, "Okay."

It was obvious she hoped Alan would come in for a while. It seemed as though Charlie didn't get many visitors.

Then she said with a cheerful tone, "The room you are looking for is the next room on the other side of the hall."

Alan said, "Cool. Thanks." Alan then whispered, "Goodbye, Charlie" and left without another word.

Charlie said, "Goodbye. Be careful this summer on the lakes."

CHAPTER 7

· · · · · · · · · ● ● ● ● ● ● ● ● ● · · · ·

VISITING CAP'N

"That's great! My grandson is going to sail on a
freighter and one that I captained," Cap'n said.

Alan continued down the hall and, on the left, found the room he wanted. He took a deep breath. Alan didn't tell Charlie or the nurse what his summer plans were. However, Charlie somehow knew that Alan might be in danger in the water on the lakes.

He entered the sterile white-walled room where his grandfather lay. "Hi, Alan" came the cheerful greeting. "It is so good to see you."

The space was similar to Charlie's, but the room had no personal items of any sort. It looked to be a place that was considered temporary for its occupant. Alan thought that his grandfather had to know he was on his deathbed.

Cap'n didn't seem to care about what else was going on in the world. He simply wanted to visit with Alan, but he also was a bit cantankerous.

"Hi, Grandpa. How are you feeling today?" Alan said without really thinking.

"I am not happy. I have cramping in my left leg," Cap'n said flatly. "The missing left leg feels like it is cramping. I know it's called phantom limb pain, but it doesn't make any sense. I have been told it's all in my head. But it hurts just like a Charlie horse."

Then he smiled and said, "When Grandma comes to visit a bit later, I think she will massage it. It will be better."

Alan wondered how his grandmother was going to massage the missing leg but didn't say anything more about it. He changed the subject.

"Well, I am off to join the crew of the *Demson* with Captain Brads," Alan initiated. "I leave tomorrow with Dad who is taking me to the South Chicago Steelworks. I will be a deckhand, but I have a Merchant Mariner's Document that lists me as a wiper as well."

"That's great! My grandson is going to sail on a freighter and one that I captained," Cap'n said. "It won't be all fun on the *Demson* although we played baseball in the hold when she was clean and empty. There will be storms and plenty of hard work."

Cap'n had a twinkle in his pale blue eyes. He said, "The Steel Company's fleet is a proud collection of boats, and the crews are outstanding and well trained. This is the same fleet that fed the Arsenal of Democracy during World War II. I served in the Coast Guard but only worked on the ore-carrying boats the entire duration of the war."

The Arsenal of Democracy was a term first used by President Franklin Roosevelt. The term was used to describe the transformation of the auto and steel industry from domestic products like automobiles to those of war like planes and tanks. Cities like Detroit were transformed during the war. The young men went to war, and their women went to work in the production plants. Over two million trucks, one hundred thousand tanks, and almost the same number of ships were built in the four years from 1941 to 1945.

As he was on a roll, Cap'n continued, "I am proud of what we did during wartime. I also wanted the best for myself. I enjoyed studying for my master's license and my engineer's license. Not an easy thing to do because you have to put in time in each position, so hardly anyone does it. I was both a chief engineer and a captain during my career. Generally, the engineer's crew and forward crew under the mates don't interact too much or ever take on each other's roles. I did and was a human bridge between them all."

"We worked hard, spent many days away from home and family, and some of us lived through some pretty violent and hard-sailing weather," reminisced the old sailor. "Some sailors drink too much. Others smoke or gamble too much. I didn't find any of these vices satisfactory to the conduct of an officer. Simply put, Alan, don't try any of these temptations."

In other words, Cap'n had seen or tried all these vices before he was an officer and had some regrets when viewing these from the perch of a responsible party dedicated to operating a productive and safe freighter. Now later in his life, his marginal actions seemed unacceptable to even him.

Cap'n lamented, "I do regret not being able to spend more time in our community back home. Of course, we had a household with your mom, her sisters, and your grandma, but I wasn't there for so much of it. I now wish I could have been more engaged in their daily lives."

Cap'n went on, "The one-hundred-plus heat in the boiler rooms during the summer were just as difficult as the windblown frigid waves on the decks in March and November. I survived both, and I can tell you, I wouldn't have it any other way. The effort to sail for me was always linked to a higher purpose.

"I was helping make steel for buildings, refrigerators, and cars. All these were expanding an American way of life for a very large number of people. More and more, people could afford to own their own car and move freely around the country as they pleased. In my lifetime, we went from horse and buggy to the moon."

The space race was a big deal. The Russians put a man in space in 1961 and right behind was the United States. However, the ultimate was a flight to the moon and back.

In 1969, less than a year before Alan and Cap'n's conversation, a lunar module landed on the moon. There were three astronauts that completed the mission to the moon. Two pilots, Aldrin and Armstrong, took the unusual-looking four-truss landing craft to the surface of the moon as the other pilot, Collins, continued to circle the orb.

When the small craft landed on the surface of the moon, it was the first to carry humans to that cold, unforgiving place. The United States' astronaut Armstrong stepped out from the ladder of the spacecraft and said, "That's one small step for man, one giant leap for mankind." Alan watched the landing on a black-and-white small-screen television late that July night, not quite a year ago.

The odyssey continued with the other astronaut disembarking and eventually saluting the planted American flag. The two men collected data and rocks before returning to the encircling spaceship. Then the three intrepid travelers returned to Earth safely. That was the ultimate in engineering.

"Yes, indeed," quipped Alan.

Cap'n had seen much in his lifetime. He worked on a farm with horses as the main method of travel either to the store or the pasture to work. Cap'n didn't like horses, and he was convinced that they didn't like him either. They were a lot of work, and farming life was difficult. Horses move more slowly when they are around people who fear them, and the scared boy who was trying to make them go quickly was not happy.

Cap' had lived through the Great Depression of the 1930s. It was a rough period as he had a family, and there was no chance of finding a different job such that he could stay home and support them. He was paid well though his wife would have liked a different way of life. His position with the Steel Company was secure due to the multiple licenses he held. He built a home during that time and actually employed laid-off crew members to work on his personal project.

Cap'n had a number of principles he lived by, such as working hard and staying the course is rewarding. He built up seniority over the years, and he was rewarded by being promoted. He was well prepared by obtaining and then maintaining his licenses. His knowledge was superior, and the relationships he built were valuable. He had a retirement account and was well compensated. He was able to captain the newest and best boats in the Steel Company's fleet. He stayed the course and was rewarded.

Another principle he followed was to depend upon your team, friends, and family. They won't let you down. The teams he put together for each of his seasons as a captain were some of the best in the industry. They could sail a huge new freighter without incident and move a massive amount of iron ore on a schedule that fed the voracious needs of the mills.

His friends supported him by being there when he needed assistance, both while he was away from home and also from boat to boat in filling his crewing needs, supplying information on the weather and general industry news. His family, although not happy with the long season away sailing, supported him through maintaining their home and family in a wonderful manner. None of these constituents ever let him down.

· · · · · · · · ● ● ● ● ● ● · · · ·

CHAPTER 8

THE VISIT CONTINUES

*Cap'n wasn't going to sugarcoat the
job as a sailor for Alan.*

Cap'n experienced World War I as a Great Lakes sailor, and then he worked in the Coast Guard during World War II, which, of course, ended with dropping of hydrogen bombs on Japan.

Cap'n was born in Grover Cleveland's second administration as president after the president had a four-year gap. He lived through both of the President Roosevelts' terms. He even knew veterans of the Civil War as a young man.

The world had change significantly during Cap'n's lifetime. Boating on the lakes didn't change much although danger was ever present, especially the weather.

No one can control the weather even if it is a bit more understandable today. It is only foreseeable in small time frames with no knowledge of exactly what the weather will be like in any specific location. Regardless of the weather, there is always a schedule to maintain as the mills are insatiable consumers in need of iron ore.

Cap'n wasn't going to sugarcoat the job as a sailor for Alan. If Alan chose this life after a summer sailing, Cap'n wanted him to be aware of the highs and, more importantly, the lows of such a choice.

"Alan, you are going to find the food on board to be plentiful, but just as important, very well prepared," Cap'n was delighted to say. "The cooks are handpicked by the captains, and their crew members are handpicked by the cook. These crews are always from the South and always have been black. It is the way the Steel Company has set it up. Be aware there are no other crew members on the boats that are black."

Alan said, "That doesn't seem right." It was almost a question.

Cap'n said curtly, "This is the way it is. I am not defending the practice, but I am explaining it." The old captain was not used to being challenged. He wasn't going to be questioned on morals by his grandson and a newly designated deckhand at that!

Alan knew it was usually impolite to challenge authority, especially his grandfather, on a topic he obviously lived through for so many years, but he also knew the being transparent in his communication at all times was something that was worthwhile practicing. Alan was shy, reserved, and never spoke a harsh word.

Alan remembered when Cap'n first retired and took him in his truck to the hardware store to buy a tool Cap'n needed for his tractor repair. The trip ended without buying anything because the store operator talked Cap'n through how to fix the problem without any additional material.

Delighted, Cap'n was in a very good mood. He looked at Alan and asked as they approached an ice-cream stand, "Do you want to stop for an ice-cream cone?" Cap'n was diabetic and probably shouldn't have ice cream.

Alan shyly said, "I don't care."

Cap'n, with an upper-handed sneer, coldly said, "I don't care either." He drove by and never said anything more about it.

Now Alan knew that being transparent in his communication at all times was important. So Alan really didn't buy into the methodology of the practice that certain jobs were designated by race. The captain could pick the African American cook, but everyone else on the cook's crew was not picked by the captain? Furthermore, the captain couldn't pick a black deckhand, wiper, or deck watch? Alan knew Captain Brads picked him mainly because he was the Cap'n's grandson. Cap'n simply didn't challenge the system, fair or not.

This set of facts had a moral dilemma at its core that showed insight about the Steel Company's leadership Alan was going to work for. Can you work for a company that has policies different than ones you would have created and embraced? Alan would need to answer that question for himself.

The trade-off between making life better for many people through the goods that are produced by the Steel Company versus not affording advancement of a whole working class of employees seemed difficult to grasp. Alan thought, *No matter how someone contracts for their services, they are full partners in the outcomes of the collective mission.*

The blacks that worked on the freighters were paid better than they would have been paid by working any other job back home. The loss of opportunity for advancement in the future versus the opportunity provided by a good job today was a difficult concept to absorb by even the cooks and the stewards currently working for the company.

However, not lost in the logic for Alan was a similar situation the old captain had found himself. Cap'n couldn't leave the job he was working, especially during the depression, even if his wife wanted him to, due to the economic setback it would cause. The captain, too, was caught in the corporate policy of being limited in advancement. The top of the Cap'n's career would be a captain, but he could expect newer and bigger vessels to navigate.

Alan would go to work for the Steel Company and be governed by the policies of the corporation but would have to think about the future of corporate America and his role in it when he graduated from engineering school in a few years.

All this would be futile thinking if he were to be drafted and had to go to war in Vietnam.

The principle here is that perfection is not a measure of success. Success comes in many forms. As time passes, more enlightenment comes with experience. The ability to change things for the better is a goal Alan will pursue over time.

Regretfully, he didn't speak his mind on the dilemma of personnel selection.

Alan wanted the change the subject, and he went back to the weather.

CHAPTER 9

• • • • • • • • • ● • • • • • • • • •

THE 1913 STORM

*"I began to cross by using the mangled steel
frame, and I was hit with an icy wave."*

Alan offered, "I heard from Mom about some violent storms on the lakes." He was hoping to be reassured about his own fear of the storms.

Alan's mom was Elm, Cap'n's daughter. She traveled from time to time in the summer with her father up and down the lakes for a week every year. She enjoyed her visits on the lakes is what she told Alan and his siblings. She hadn't seen much of Cap'n for any extended period until he retired, with exception of the couple of months in the winter from Christmas to the end of February or on those summer jaunts. She had never visited Cap'n on a voyage when there was a violent storm and really had no idea what the experience was like.

Alan continued, "What was the worst storm you experienced?"

"Well, let me mull this over, but this is an easy question," Cap'n said as he furrowed and then raised his brow. "The year was 1913 in November and I was twenty, brash, and six feet tall. The Big Blow was a blizzard and tornado combined. The thirty-five-foot waves were coming over the bow and running over the top of the boat. The deck was flooded with water, and it looked like there was only a forward cabin and an aft cabin with a smokestack. Nothing was in clear view between the two edifices of nearly five hundred feet. The waves came in short quick spacing, and wind seemed to blow opposite of the wave action. My boat was between Lexington and Port Austin on Lake Huron. We were trying to take shelter near the shoreline, along with several other freighters. Our boat began to buckle due to the side hammer of the waves. We were dead in the water, maybe a half mile out. Other boats nearby were sounding their horns, but we couldn't see anything between the waves and the blizzard's snow. We were completely blinded by the snow and darkness. We had lost power, and the entire electrical system on board was out of service. We didn't have lights, except for battery-powered torches and kerosene lanterns.

"I dimly saw what I thought I could make out of the aft crew members beginning to make the lifeboats ready to launch as the captain ordered us to abandon ship. As the crew loosened the starboard lifeboat, it broke free and was lost in the dark waters with two crew members in tow. Several crew members from the forward cabins of the boat tried to make their way on deck to the aft of the freighter. They were picked off the deck quickly and permanently in their attempt to escape the boat.

"Next came an effort for the remaining forward crew members to make their way along the inside passageway next to the hull. They were without light, and between the hulls, there were steel hatchways to pass through. The crew made their way to about halfway along the four-hundred-foot boat's inner passageway and found the hull bent to such a degree that they could not pass through the mangled steel. These men would not be able to turn around before the midship came apart. All the forward crew either lost their lives on deck or part of the failed effort of trying to go to the aft of the freighter by way of the inside passageway."

Alan was transfixed with the retelling of the shipwreck. "Weren't you a forward crew member? How did you make it to the lifeboat? What did you do?"

Cap'n recalled, "I began to follow the crew down the starboard side of that passage way that had bent steel bracings and plates, and then I remembered that the only lifeboat remaining was being launched from the port side, and it was nearest the shore. The other lifeboat was lost already in the storm.

"I didn't go far down the starboard side before I decided to turn around. I called for the others ahead of me, but no one listened or," Cap'n said reverently, "maybe they didn't hear me. I knew the port side had opened up and water was rushing into the holds. I decided that I was strong, and I would try to climb over the missing walkway by the use of the steel bracing inside the hull on that breeched port side."

Cap'n was thoughtful but with honor and said, "This was a fortunate decision for me, but not without its difficulties."

Sometimes not deciding on a course of action too quickly is the best choice. This was true for Cap'n on that day. If he would have decided to follow the crew down to first passageway, he would have been lost in the storm.

Thinking about the options and his capability to manage through the difficulty made the decision easier, especially with the additional information about the lifeboat conditions. The hull opening was a deterrent factor but one that when the decision was made was worth the risk.

"I had a flashlight which helped me maneuver the passageway. I made it to the midship and found the gapping breach about ten feet wide. Water was quickly moving in as each successive wave hit. The steel bracing was a tangled mess over the gap. I began to cross by using the mangled steel frame, and I was hit with an icy wave.

"I was frozen with fear and the shock of the wave. I lost my light in the heavy water surge, but I held on tight as the water rushed back out. I collected myself, and then I proceeded alone in the dark.

"In front of me, I felt there was a gap with no steel bracing. When I reached across the gap, another wave hit. It felt like a sledgehammer, but I was committed to not let go. I leaped as the wave receded, and my hands gabbed the steel on the other side.

"All this occurred without any vision. In this experience, I was more afraid than I have ever been. I was alone, in the dark, wet, cold, and bruised from the water and the steel. At that moment, though, I knew I had made it past the opening. I had hope."

Cap'n was tiring. So Allan suggested that he was satisfied with the story ending at that point.

Cap'n was not ready to finish and pressed on, "I made my way alone and in the dark through the hull passageway to the opening at the aft end of the freighter. Water was rushing down the passageway from the stairs above as the boat had had taken on enough water to be submerged to the main deck.

"I fought my way past the onrush of water up and to the opening on the deck. Through the door, I saw the last of the aft crew dropping the lifeboat to the lake below. I rushed to the pendant and rigging. As I peered over the edge, the small boat was being battered by the waves against the hull of the freighter.

"I shouted down to the lifeboat, but no one heard me. No one looked up! I looked around and found a piece of the rigging block. I threw it down to the waterline, bouncing it off the edge of the lifeboat. It splashed into the water next to the life raft. The crew looked up. They shouted for me to jump. I jumped maybe twenty feet into the water next to the boat without a life jacket. It was cold, and I was frozen. I couldn't move my arms or my legs. One of the black stewards pulled me into the lifeboat and gave me a life vest.

"There were only ten members of the crew of twenty-eight that had made it into the small craft. As we pulled on the oars toward what we thought was shore, we could see the ship had come apart and sink. The sinking took maybe an hour after it hit the rocks.

"I was lucky to be alive.

"The closer we got to shore, the waves were rising and falling and ripping at the lifeboat. Then the small boat capsized! Again, I found myself in the frigid water, and because I was already very cold and wet, my muscles didn't go stiff this time. I was still a long way from shore, and there were no lights on land.

"Later, I heard that the on-shore electric infrastructure had been destroyed by the blizzard and the wind. But I could hear horns from the large vessels behind me, and I found my bearing to go the opposite way. Eventually, I could make out twinkling in front of me. I thought that I was dead and that I was seeing the lights of heaven. What I learned later was that they were car lights on shore. I swam toward the lights. This was the turning point. I had hope, and it helped me keep moving toward land. The waves were huge, and the wind was unbearable. I swam about nine hundred yards in the darkness and arrived on the small rocks at the beach. There were people immediately on shore to help me, and they took me to a local doctor."

Cap'n softly said, "The next day, I went home, not too far away, in Port Huron, where I learned of the deaths of twenty-four of my shipmates, with only four of us surviving. Six men died after the lifeboat turned over. They didn't make the swim to shore. I was the only forward crew member to make it back alive. There were many other boats with similar and sad results from that Big Blow."

Alan said, "I am so glad you made it through that ordeal alive. If you didn't, I wouldn't be here either."

Cap'n said, "That's right, Alan. Let's call it fate."

Alan thought a change of subject might be a good idea. He thought a moment.

Alan said, "I remember when we were going up to your cottage when I was about ten. President Kennedy's funeral was underway, and Mom and Grandma went up north earlier in the day in grandma's car. We waited for Dad to get off work. Then Dad, me, and the other two kids went up together with you in our car. We stopped on the way for dinner at a really nice place. Our family almost never went out to eat, and therefore it was something really special."

Cap'n said, "I remember the trip and timing."

Alan went on, "As we went into the restaurant, I asked Dad who was paying. He didn't answer. When we were taken to our table and seated, you took the head of the table. I remember being nervous about what were the correct table manners, including the right utensils to use, the placement of the napkin, and—most worrisome—what to order. When we got the menu, I looked at Dad as if to say, what can we order?"

Alan then said gently, "You saw our concern and Dad's fidgeting, and then you simply put everyone at ease. Your words were so refreshing and comforting. You said, 'I want you all to know that I brought you into this restaurant, and I want you to know I am paying for this meal. You can order anything on the menu and as much as you like.'"

"My only rule," Cap'n said in a bit of a singsong voice, "is that you need to eat everything you order. Oh, by the way, save room for desert."

Alan said, "I respect you for that moment of generosity. You not only took the worry and unconscious burden away from everyone at the table but also you also made everyone at ease for the rest of the trip. Thank you."

Cap'n said, "You're welcome. You have great instincts."

Cap'n looked up and said, "Here's Grandma."

She was a small woman but had a big heart. She smiled when Cap'n asked, "I hope you can help me with my leg."

Grandmother, like Grandfather, was of German descent. She was stoic and somewhat distant. She was disappointed in the solitary life of a sailor's wife and, at times, reflected it in her demeanor. She was not pleased with Alan's impending job on a freighter. She worried about the potential that he would choose the life of a sailor.

Alan said, "Hi, Grandma. I am glad to see you."

Grandma said, "Hi, Alan. How has your visit with Cap'n been going? Has he told you all about the boats?"

Alan replied, "The storms, the food, and the crew make the life on a boat for the summer an adventure. I am not sure that it will be a lifelong career for me, but I do want to experience it once."

Then Alan gathered himself. Alan said, "I love you both, but I have gotta go buy some boots for the summer."

"Have a great summer on the lakes," Alan's grandmother said as she turned to attend to her husband.

Alan walked down the hallway and out into the receding light of the day. He was sad to leave his two grandparents. It was an enlightening visit, and it added to suspense of the next day.

He got into his Studebaker and was welcomed by the Beatles' "Let It Be" on the radio. Alan sang along as he drove home. "And in my hour of darkness, she is standing right in front of me, speaking words of wisdom. Let it be."

He drove to Kmart and bought work boots for the summer. Then he went home.

PREPARATION TO LEAVE HOME

The car was loaded with maps on the front seat, Alan's
duffel bag in the trunk, and the food on the back seat.

The next day, Alan and his dad, Ham, were up early and packing the family's '66 Chevy Bel Air for a journey from Port Huron, Michigan, to Chicago, Illinois. Dad would drive seven hours to the South Chicago slip at the steelworks and immediately return the same day. This was a grueling trip, but one that was worth it to everyone involved.

Alan could earn a good summer's wage with room and board. This would take pressure off the family budget. Alan ate like a starving young lion at every meal and could drink a gallon of milk daily. Alan's mom, Elm, did his laundry and cleaned the house, including his room. He had no secrets from his mom. Although Alan appreciated his family, he didn't fully realize the financial and time-consuming burden he placed on them.

Alan was studying to be a civil engineer. Ham thought Alan could become a surveyor. Alan was encouraged by Cap'n who was licensed as an engineer and all executive positions through captain. Alan knew his grandfather earned a great living and thought he might be able to do the same over his lifetime. A licensed engineer could command a good salary, and there would be work at a steady pace if he wanted to work hard.

The cost of college was expensive with books and supplies, including transportation, tuition, and laboratory fees. Dad was paying for Alan's food and the roof over his head.

While Alan had just finished his freshman year at engineering school, he worked twenty hours per week as a stock clerk in the college bookstore. The job didn't pay well but was very convenient, logistically. The pay from the job contributed to payment of some of his school expenses as Ham and Elm did not have the resources to pay for any of his school costs. The first year had almost drained Alan's entire life savings, including high school graduation gifts and birthday money from over the years. The job on a freighter was a godsend.

Alan didn't have a scholarship or grants and loans as Ham wouldn't fill out the paperwork. Ham was concerned he would be responsible somehow for the repayment. Ham did have a bit of distrust that Alan could and would be successful after college. "You're smart in school, but you're gonna flunk life," he would say.

Ham had lived through the Great Depression of the 1930s. People lost their homes due to debt. Ham didn't have a mortgage as he built his own home piecemeal over a three-year period after he came back from the war. Ham didn't have any debt, no credit cards or loans. He was committed to keep it that way.

The family had a long history with suspicion of owing a bank, the government, or anyone else. This was historically true for the family as long ago as the American Civil War of the 1860s.

The war was protracted, and volunteers were not as plentiful as needed. A disliked policy of conscription or a draft was put in place by Congress. It became even more unpopular when wealthy men could hire a substitute to serve in their place. This avoided the concern with the constitutional promise of the "pursuit of happiness."

In Alan's family, a great uncle was paid to fulfill a soldier's obligation to join the Army, and the money he earned helped save the family from losing their home, farm, and livelihood. That uncle was sent to Texas to fight the Confederacy where he died from a malaria infection.

However, for the best, the money was used to pay the tax lien on the family farm and save it for posterity. This story was passed down through the generations to drive home the point of not owing anyone anything, period.

Therefore, to take on debt was considered an extremely dire decision. The purpose of college attendance was to educate, which, in turn, would help you to become better off in life. College itself was not supposed to put you and your family at risk of becoming worse off. "Neither a debtor or a bowered be" from Shakespeare's *Hamlet* was Ham's motto. I know he learned this from his parents, especially his mother.

It had been wonderful that Alan had never lived anywhere but in his childhood home. It was also restricting and narrow-minded. His father had built the house without a loan after World War II when he returned to Wadhams in 1945. Ham married Alan's mother, Elm, and built their home on the same family farm acreage as Cap'n and Grandma. Elm and Ham had three children: the oldest a girl and then the two boys.

Alan was a second child, but with this summer job, he would move into a position at the time of being more experienced and more resilient than either of his siblings, Carol and Bert.

Alan had many typical youthful experiences with public school activities, family camping throughout the United States, and working with Ham on their house maintenance, their church construction, and the odd painting job for friends. None of these were paid opportunities for Alan.

Even with friends and in sports, he would be called overly trusting and a bit naive. Alan was very much like the main character in a book he read in high school titled *Candide* by a French author named Voltaire. Candide had a perspective on everything he experienced as being "the best of all possible worlds."

Alan's life would change dramatically over the next three months. He would become worldlier, less reserved, and ultimately, a more hardened man.

Alan packed a duffel bag with clothes sufficient for a week. These were mainly jeans, shirts, underwear, and socks. He bought a new pair of boots the previous day; he would wear them on the ride to the boat. Finally, he shoved in with his gear a couple of sweatshirts, a Detroit Tigers baseball cap, a small Bible and a coat.

Alan would have to learn to do his laundry on the freighter although Elm had instructed him several times on load size and detergent amounts. Even so, Alan was clueless but confident.

Ham packed nothing. He simply wasn't going to stay anywhere during the trip. This was a cost-effective decision, but not a safety-first concept. It will all work out, but it is a simple demonstration of Ham's cost-conscience attitude.

This was going to be a grueling sixteen-hour ordeal, with two seven-hour drives, breaks for food, relief and gas, and a quick tour of the boat with Alan. They couldn't leave any earlier as they were meeting the *Demson* in Chicago at a specific time of two in the afternoon, central time. Additionally, Ham had to go to work the next day.

Elm emerged from the kitchen and into the driveway with a box labeled Wonder Bread. She had procured the free box from the grocery store the day before just for this trip. It was full of food for the trip to Chicago for Alan and Ham. There was enough for Dad's return trip home.

The box contained sandwiches, apples and bananas, chips, homemade pickles, and cookies. Water and coffee were the drinks of choice in the thermoses. She handed the box to Ham, and he promptly put it in the Chevy.

The car was loaded with maps on the front seat, Alan's duffel bag in the trunk, and the food on the back seat. Ham had filled the car with gas the night before, and the car was ready to go.

"Mom, I am off to work," Alan quipped. He was in a good mood.

They hugged, and she whispered, "Be safe." She knew he was in for a big awakening.

Alan said boldly, "I will."

In Elm's mind, she was unsettled and wistful but put on a brave face for the two travelers. She wanted Alan to go. She wanted Ham to be safe.

Alan hugged Carol and hit Bert on the arm. None of the siblings had tears. Alan hopped in the car with Ham. He left the keys to the Studebaker for his two siblings to use as they wished during the summer when he was away.

CHAPTER 11

ON THE RIDE TO CHICAGO

Ham said, "None of it. The history of
this conflict is long and tortuous."

As the car pulled out of the driveway, a sadness began to over-whelm Alan. He was melancholy as he teared up and looked out the passenger-side window. The tearful thought wasn't about leaving because he knew he would return in a few months, but it was about his youth disappearing in the rearview mirror. He would miss the times of sitting around the table in the evening and discussing everything from politics to the next great thing his dad was thinking about or the day's activities and work. The boyhood games and toys were no longer to be part of his future, only his past. He knew he wouldn't ever want to play with them again as he did before this ride.

Friends and youth activity would be a distant thought through the summer. These would even fade from importance as the summer events unfolded, he thought. He didn't get to say goodbye to any of these important people in his life. He didn't even get to say goodbye to Dad's parents, Alan's grandparents. This was sad.

Ham tried to lift the spirits of Alan. Ham started, "I know you like Bill Cosby's humor. Well, I had a boyhood comic that I really liked. His name was Will Rogers, and he was a humorist and critic of politicians, the federal government, and the Congress. He died when

I was just a kid in an airplane crash in Alaska with a famous aviator named Wiley Post.

"Some of his sayings were just common sense but really funny. These are some of my favorites: Always drink upstream from the herd. In other words, get ahead of the crowd but also don't drink water the cattle were bathing in or using as a toilet.

"If you want to know how a man stands, go among the people who are in the same business. Does he treat his competitors with dignity and his customers fairly?

"Even if you're on the right track, you'll get run over if you just sit there. He could be talking about a railroad track, or he could be simply saying, get moving to make something good happen."

"One more?" Ham concluded. "Try to live your life so that you wouldn't be afraid to sell the family parrot to the town gossip. In other terms, live the same way in private as you would in public. Be an honest and kind family man."

Alan said, "I guess being a moral man is a crucial part of how to conduct all activity. Nothing seems to be a secret."

As Alan reached for the dial on the radio, Ham said quietly, "No. I don't want to listen to rock and roll even if it is popular with all your friends, your sister, and her friends. I have the news on, and as we go, we might find a Western music station we can both live with." Ham turned up the volume a bit.

The news on the radio broke the discussion, and their conversation ceased. The announcer dryly continued talking, "President Nixon today held a news conference. The defense of his decision to move troops into Cambodia was his subject. The troops would likely be in Cambodia for eight months training South Vietnam forces. The war would be shortened by this action said Nixon. He added that one hundred fifty thousand soldiers would return by next spring."

Ham said, "I don't believe it."

Alan retorted, "What don't you believe? Going into Cambodia to train Vietnam soldiers or bringing back one hundred fifty thousand troops?"

Ham said, "None of it. The history of this conflict is long and tortuous."

He went on, "In my war, the French were swept away in Vietnam by the Japanese in March 1945. The Japanese placed a puppet leader in the country to make it look like it was independent. By August of that year, Roosevelt had died, Truman dropped the nuclear bombs, Japan surrendered, and Vietnam had overthrown the puppet leader."

Ham went on, "By September of 1945, the British came to Vietnam to restore peace and reestablish it as a French colony. The Vietnamese wanted the United States to recognize the new independent government which the United States didn't do. The United States was an ally of both the French and the British as you know.

"By the spring of 1946, the north and south of Vietnam were split between the new independent government in the North and the French government in the South. By 1948 and into 1949, the North was recognized by China. The South was then released as a colony by the French but was still loyal to the French. It was recognized by the United States and the western European countries. By 1950, we were giving military aid to South Vietnam and provided military advisors."

Alan made the connection. "Dad these events were a direct outcome of the post–World War II alignments. The Vietnam War effort began in the 1950s?"

"That's right," Ham replied. "When our current president was vice president under Eisenhower, he stated that he supported troop intervention, but it was considered an unpopular decision to do so. By 1959, our military advisors were being killed in Vietnam, and in President Kennedy's term in 1961, military deaths were realized."

Now Ham was getting to his point. "From then to now, there has been a rise in troops in Vietnam to over five hundred thousand. About two years ago, over five hundred young soldiers just like you died in a week. Then last winter, a draft lottery was instituted. I know there was a draft in World War II as well. But we understood that our country had been attacked. It is not the case with Vietnam."

Ham stated flatly, "They promised me that if I fought in Southeast Asia, we would win and our sons, like you, Alan, would never have to fight there again. Nuts!" Ham was welling up. "I believed them then, but I don't anymore."

The two men stopped for a restroom break, to buy some gas, and to eat some of the food Elm prepared. Alan was fatigued from the conversation. This was serious, and the message was clear.

As the car moved on through Kalamazoo, the topic returned.

Ham said, "You know, Mom and Grandma's family is from Ontario. You could go to Canada instead of going into the draft. Think about it."

Alan had three more years before his S2 classification as a student would be lost. It was considered a rich kid's deferment, but it certainly was not true in Alan's case. The war seemed to be winding down, but it was a huge risk. As a graduate engineer, he probably wouldn't be on the military front lines like Ham, who was as a paratrooper. There was the draft lottery this summer for his birth year, and if by chance he won a large number, maybe over one hundred fifty, he wouldn't likely be drafted. If he were drafted, he would go and serve. When he returned, he would have the GI Bill to help pay for tuition.

Alan thought how important it was to understand how global, national, state, and local activities affected how people lived and even businesses operated. He was working through a maze of inputs as to how to move through his life and still meet his goals of a college degree and a good-paying position when he graduated.

Alan said, "I am an American and couldn't imagine not living in America. If I must go into the Army, maybe I can go into the Army Corps of Engineers."

Ham smiled and said, "That would make me proud."

He turned on the country music station, and we listened and then sang along with Johnny Cash. "Daddy sang bass, mama sang tenor, me and little brother would join right in there."

CHAPTER 12

BASEBALL AND LIFE

"There was magic in being at a major-league
baseball game and spending that day with you."

Alan carefully, while eyeing his dad, switched the radio channel from country music to the Detroit Tigers game. The
Tigers were ahead against the Washington Senators. "The
Tigers don't seem to have much of a chance to be very good this
year," Ham said. "It doesn't seem like we can do anything against the
Orioles or the Yankees this year. Additionally, we seem to be quite
average against everyone else. I bet we end up below five hundred
this year."

"I couldn't agree more," said Alan. "It could be that Willie
Horton will be the only player who might hit over three hundred.
Hard to watch after the recent great seasons, especially in 1968."

Ham agreed and said, "It is always good for the Tigers to win
a World Series, but it was especially rewarding to the whole state of
Michigan after the '67 riots in Detroit. Upon reflection, it seemed to
be a good way to heal as a community, at least a little bit."

Ham waxed on, "By the way, my favorite player when I was
your age was Charley Gehringer. He was automatic at second base
and a local guy from Fowlerville here in Michigan. He's a Hall of
Famer. He's still alive, and I think he lives nearby in Bloomfield Hills
today."

Ernie Harwell, one of the announcers of the game, continued with, "It is a good outing for the Tigers as they are ahead one to nothing after two innings played. The Tigers campaign is now at seventeen wins and eighteen loses. They have only won two of their last ten games."

Alan exhaled and said, "Let's turn off the radio."

Alan said, "Man, I love baseball. I remember when I was in Little League, the whole team and their parents went down to Tiger Stadium. You and I sat in left field not too many rows up. I could actually see Rocky Colavito's face. I couldn't have been happier that day. There was magic in being at a major-league baseball game and spending that day with you."

Ham replied, "I remember it well. You became quite a ballplayer yourself. Baseball reflects life. On the grandest level, a bunch of people separate themselves into teams and compete the entire 162-game season. Some teams play, don't measure up, and they don't make the playoffs. Other teams compete in the playoffs and then, one by one, lose a series such that there is only one winner in the end. There is just one champion and only one trophy."

Understanding the logic, Ham pressed, "On another level, each team has its heroes. The players that are most popular tend to be open and show their emotions. They also seem to me to be good sports and kindhearted people. These men make it easy to see yourself through them. They are also very skilled playing their position and often are the reason the whole team does well."

Without a stop, Ham rattled on, "On a deeper level, each game is played with an optimism and an expectation of winning. Each day through the season and every scheduled game provides a new start. The baseball game has rules, rule keepers called umpires, and scores and statistics are kept throughout the game and for posterity. There will be a winner, but we don't know who it will be until the last out is made."

Insightfully Ham explained, "For example, in 1901, the Tigers played their first game of their inaugural season. They were behind, 3-4, entering the ninth inning against the Milwaukee Brewers. Fans were everywhere, including on the field, due to a sellout. The crowd was pressing in, and their taunts and yells intimidated the opposing pitchers. Great hitting and base running by the Tigers helped them to pull out a win. I remember hearing about the headlines attributed to the *Detroit Tribune*. The newspaper purportedly reported that there was a tumultuous celebration after the game. The crowd didn't have to go far to swamp the players in their joy."

With thoughtfulness, Ham took a moment and gathered his thoughts and then began again, "Deeper yet, each player has a role on every pitch. The player has an opportunity to make something special happen. An out, a strike, a last pitch for a perfect game, or a walk off home run are all opportunities for each player every time he is in the game. The player can be a scapegoat or a star, and even be remembered for just that one play for his entire career."

"Look," Ham reported, "Babe Ruth is remembered as a scapegoat for an attempted steal in the final World Series game in 1926, which became their final out to lose the game and the series to the Cardinals. But he is best remembered as the greatest of all-time home run hitter with 60 dingers in the 1927 season, over 40 in eleven different seasons, and 714 in his career."

Finally Ham stopped with, "A life principle I have modeled for myself over the years is you can be successful with the team you have. Not everyone on a team has the same skills and background. In fact, it is important to have differences among your teammates. The more diversity, the better chance that someone will have an ability, knowledge, or experience that everyone will benefit from at exactly the right time."

Ham said, "Okay, do you know that during World War II baseball continued to be played, but not everyone avoided the war? Over five hundred major leaguers served in the war. Could you imagine being in the same military squadron with Ted Williams, Hank Greenberg, or Joe DiMaggio? I think it was great that they didn't stay back home in safety and celebrity. It was even better that they began to serve in the middle of their careers and lives, just like so many of us."

With a smile Ham clicked, "With President Roosevelt giving the green light, baseball continued through the war years, and I believe it gave working men and women a wholesome activity that was American through and through."

Alan was impressed with the depth of the thinking his dad described in his baseball philosophy.

Alan said, "Thank you. That was both enlightening and deeply personal." He paused and took a deep breath. "Not to change the subject back to the war again, but can you tell me about your experience during the war?"

Ham shook his head. He didn't want to talk about it.

Alan persisted. "Dad, you stated that they lied to you and you wanted me to dodge the draft and go to Canada. Why is it so difficult to talk about?" pressed Alan.

CHAPTER 13

· · · · · · · · · ● · · · · · · · · ·

PREPARATION FOR WAR

*Alan pressed again, "Tell me
something real and personal."*

When Ham left home, it was in a similar way to how Alan is leaving home now. The difference was Ham was going to war. He was twenty-two in February 1943. A little over a year earlier, the Japanese bombed Pearl Harbor, December 7, 1941, a day that will live in infamy based upon a speech by President Roosevelt.

Ham had been working at the railroad since graduating from high school. He was good at his job, and he helped tremendously on the family farm, which still used horses to plow the fields. In fact, when he joined the Army, his first pay went to help buy a tractor so Grandpa could still get the work done without him and his brother.

His father, Alan's grandfather, took him to the train five miles away in Port Huron, heading south for Fort Wayne in Detroit. He wished his son well. It was a sad day for everyone. Ham was assigned to the Eleventh Airborne with eight thousand other soldiers. His commander was Major General Joe May Swing from New Jersey. After orientation and a health checkup, he traveled from Detroit to North Carolina for basic training under Colonel Orin "Hard Rock" Haugen from Wyoming. This was very typical training with an emphasis on physical fitness and weapons ability.

Ham could do over two hundred push-ups at a time. He wasn't the best in this category because he told of a soldier in his squadron who could do over six hundred push-ups at a time. Alan could only do fifty-two in a high school physical education class which was second best among his classmates.

Ham shot rifles on the farm at home and occasionally chased way unwanted varmints from the chickens and crops. In the Army, he became a marksman. He won recognition and was rewarded for this skill.

He then went on to Georgia as the training intensified. Ham was in a parachute infantry regiment, the 511th. Ham trained as a paratrooper in the heat and humidity. At first, he jumped from a 250-foot-tall free platform and then graduated to the air and jumped from a plane. Ham was designated as the radioman for his platoon. This meant he had an additional burdened of thirty-eight pounds of electronics gear to carry on his back.

Ham started softly, "We were prepared at multiple levels for the various outcome possibilities that might occur. We trained at night, in the rain, and without sleep. We even trained with live ammunition. We acted like everyone was against us and we only had one another who we trusted with our lives."

Ham opened up, "There was more to training than just physical ability. We had to be smart and not let our emotions take over even when we were under duress. We held planning sessions with small changes in facts that kept us making new assessments of the situation and what each soldier would do in that new circumstance."

The next stop in the United States was Louisiana where they were checked out like a final examination. They covered ten miles in an hour with one hundred pounds of gear on their backs in the swamps of the bayou. It was in the winter, but tough nonetheless.

After a year of training, they went to California for transfer to the Pacific in May 1944. They specifically were on their way to New Guinea on the transport *Sea Pike*. None of this training was easy, but the hard stuff was yet to come.

In 1942, General MacArthur left the Philippines, promising to return. The Philippines were a protectorate of the United States prior to the Japanese aggression of 1942. Ham and his compatriot soldiers helped fulfill the return promise.

Alan pressed again, "Tell me something real and personal."

Ham said, "Okay. We trained and trained until we were told we were going to New Guinea as we left our base near San Francisco, California. The transport was horrible. We were crowded in group quarters, and the food was barely edible. We were trained and fit, so the trip was long and boring with limited exercise and movement.

"When we arrived in New Guinea, we began to train for fitness, weaponry, and the climate. It was a jungle, and the swaps were not easy to manage. It was humid, and the mosquitoes were voracious. However, I think it was no coincidence that the division commander's middle name had a familiar ring to it. I had fate on my side."

CHAPTER 14

WAR IS AWFUL

"Day after day, soldiers I trained with lost their lives."

H am continued with an earnest tone, "We left for Leyte, Philippines, by ship in November. It was hot and very muggy. Then the weather turned wet, and the rain came down in a deluge. It was our first deployment action, and everyone was anxious, and I could easily say…afraid. I and some other guys were praying and writing letters to our families back home. We didn't know what to expect.

"We could hear gunfire as soon as we arrived. We were organized and immediately ordered to go through the steep hillsides we could see from the landing point. The hills and ravines supported forests where the enemy laid in wait. The fighting was sporadic, but I saw my friends and fellow soldiers being picked off. Some died, and others were horribly wounded. It was terrifying and it was awful.

"It rained and rained, maybe a couple of feet of rain over just a few days. We ran out of food and ammunition, and therefore, at times, small planes made emergency drops for us. But the toughest thing of all were wet socks. Your feet simply rotted.

"After days of fighting and slow movement, we finally made it to the other side of the island, but we had lost a lot of men. I lost my best friend, Bud. It is tough seeing someone you are fighting along-side suddenly be killed. I was no longer a simple guy from a small farm near Port Huron. We set up camp for about a month before we had to go again.

"We deployed to Luzon in waves by air in early February 1945. I was in the second wave. We dropped by parachute off course by more than a mile and had to quickly return to the planned landing spot. Running for your life with all that gear was difficult. One of the guys kept saying keep your head down as he popped up and down to see what was down field. The third time he popped up, he was shot in the head. *Just follow your orders and you will be safe,* I kept saying to myself.

"After what seemed like hours, we were all landed. We were headed toward Manila. As we arrived near the city, the Japanese had constructed heavy blockhouses for protection which contained large guns and mortars. After fifteen days of fighting and many dead and wounded soldiers, we finally completed the task of taking the city. This is when I lost most of my buddies. I especially miss Jack and Ray. They were good men. Day after day, soldiers I trained with lost their life. A total of maybe five hundred men lost their lives in the war and another six hundred were wounded.

"By the way, during this particular battle, we heard President Roosevelt had died. It was tough to think that the commander in chief was dead, but then again, so were a lot of the soldiers I was fighting with. Thankfully, this fighting ended in May.

"Believe it or not, we ended up doing refresher training over the next few weeks, and of course, we were in a tent camp, where nothing ever dried out. Now that's the Army. I think they didn't want us becoming aware of the pretty girls and the local food and drink."

Alan knew his father as an honest and decent man. Alan stopped his dad, "What did—"

Ham soldiered on, "By the end of June, we continued south, clearing out the enemy. I was on the ground until we had a final parachute jump into a place called Aparri. The jump was messed up, and a couple of guys were killed while landing and another fifty or so got hurt on the terrain with tough high winds. We took the final ground, but more of my friends died. Hard Rock Haugen was mortally wounded and died in battle in the Philippines."

Alan asked reverently, "Did you shoot anyone?"

Ham simply replied, "I was cited many times for exemplary conduct in ground combat against an armed enemy. I took spoils of war from dead soldiers, which is illegal. Everyone seemed to do it. I am not proud that I participated. A samurai sword was my prize, and it is still in our house back home. I am still a bit sorry for doing so. The family of the samurai believe past warriors live through the sword. There is a family who is now incomplete after centuries of passing the sword down to the next generation. Don't think you can make something illegal somehow legal.

"We did have an adventure though. A few of us went out in the jungle to make sure there were no enemy stragglers. We heard the crushing of trees and grunting noises. We thought we were about see a band of soldiers. So we hid on the side of a clearing. Out of the jungle came a dinosaur, ten feet long and weighed maybe three hundred pounds. It is called a Komodo dragon, we found out later.

"I got Malaria and didn't really understand it. The mosquitoes were everywhere, and we all had welts. I wasn't diagnosed until I got to Japan. I was still a private although I had been up and down the chain to sergeant and back. I didn't always meet the expectations of the command."

Alan stopped his dad again, "Okay, what did you do?"

Ham paused, thought better of it, and then said, "Really nothing much. By August 6 and then 9, atomic bombs were dropped on Japan. We were sent to occupy Japan by the end of August 1945. We landed in Okinawa and, a few weeks later, were transported by air to Yokohama. We took a train to our base and ended up stopping in a tunnel while the smoke from the engine filled the train. We all nearly died by accident in that tunnel after all the enemy fighting.

"I was immediately sent to the hospital with a fever due to malaria. While I was there, the hospital started on fire. I jumped from a second-story window onto concrete and broke both of my ankles. I was in recovery for months, but I became a master at checkers and pretty good at chess. When I was done, I went home for Christmas. Dreams do come true."

Just like baseball, war had its champion in the end. The individual teams had winners and losers, its heroes and its goats. The individual soldiers were successful on one day and on other days wounded or killed. Those soldiers that lived on carried the dismay and the glory. These individual men made history.

"Alan, I simply don't want to talk about the worst time in my life. I believed them when they said you fight and you win so your sons do not have to go to war, especially in the South Pacific. Vietnam is in the South Pacific!"

Ham was spent. Alan was grateful that he had the time to share this first insight into his dad as a soldier.

Alan said almost imperceptibly, "Okay."

· · · · · · · · ●●●● ● ●●●● · · · · · ·

CHAPTER 15

CHICAGO AND THE EMBARKING

Briggs laughed and said, "I was a young deckhand when I first met your grandfather, Cap'n."

The drive was silent for a while. Alan and Ham made it through Indiana; they passed the exit to Gary where they both noted that there were steel factories. The air had the smell of sulfur, like rotten eggs.

It wasn't long when they entered Illinois and exited the freeway for South Chicago. As they drove through the city streets toward the lakeshore, the large buildings looked old, unkempt, and tired. The streets were dirty and the grit of the iron-making process was evident everywhere. The structures wore the output of the steel-making process. No one walked the sidewalks, and the place looked completely worn-out.

Alan broke the silence, "Yuck. This is depressing."

Ham said, "Yes, and a bit unreal. It won't be far, maybe a dozen blocks or so. We should be able to see the docks and a place to park the car in a bit."

As they drove on, the father and the son felt similarly both sad and optimistic. The car pulled up to the steelworks of South Chicago. The guard at the gate asked what they wanted, and upon explanation, he directed the car to a visitor parking spot next to the gate. Alan and Ham got out with the duffel bag. They were given directions to go through the steel mill to the other side of the works and then out one of the large doors.

Alan said, "I can't believe that we can just walk through this plant. We don't have any safety gear. We don't really know what we're doing, and there isn't any escort or guide. We weren't given any simple safety instructions. I see massive pots of hot liquid ore which has to be over two thousand degrees!"

A few moments later, Alan explained, "These molten cauldrons are so hot I can feel the heat from over fifty yards away. How do we know what not to touch?"

The two visitors saw silhouettes of men working at the large equipment at the very edge of the massive kettles of ore. The building was dark except for the fiery molten iron.

Ham raised his voice and said flatly, "Don't touch anything. Let's move as quickly as we can and make it out of this plant."

Alan said, "Okay, but it is a very interesting, dark, and frightening place."

Alan felt a hot breeze across his face as they walked out into the falling sunlight of the late afternoon.

The men looked in both directions down the half-mile-long docks and saw the *Demson* moored to spars a few hundred yards away. She was built in 1918 and was 580 feet long. She had burned iron ore red paint on her hull with silver stripes on a black smokestack.

As they approached the vessel, it was almost completely unloaded, and the main deck was high off the water. There was a ladder attached to the boat's side that seemed to stretch fifty feet up and was at a very steep angle.

At the top of the ladder came a hello. It was the first mate, Ken Briggs, wearing a huge smile, a short sleeve shirt, sunglasses, and a ball cap. He said, "Come aboard. Do you need help with your bag?"

Alan said, "I don't think so" and started to ascend the ladder. He had to hold on to the ladder rail with one hand and hold the heavy bag with the other. This was tricky business and dangerous, but he didn't want a failure of his first task. He struggled but managed to get to the top without incident.

Briggs gave Alan a hearty handshake and then took off his glasses and welcomed Ham on board. Briggs laughed and said, "I was a young deckhand when I first met your grandfather, Cap'n. I know that this experience is new and maybe bit frightening. Don't worry and we will make you right at home."

This introduction was as much for Ham as it was for Alan. It was reassuring and comfortable.

"Let me show you to your quarters," Briggs pressed. "It won't be long, and we will be on our way."

They walked across the deck to the port side of the boat and up the deck to the forward bulkhead. Then they went through the door and down the steel steps to the deck below. The area was complete with the bosun's cabin, bathroom with a shower, a laundry, and storage lockers for paint and tools. The open room was large, and just off to one side was the deckhand bunk room. Alan peered in. No one was there.

Briggs said abruptly, "The other guys are working the lines. Why don't you dump your gear? You can work out your bunk and dresser assignments when you meet the other deckhands after they are finished."

"Well, it's time to go, Ham," Briggs proclaimed. Alan and Ham followed the first mate back up the stairs and across the ore-covered decks to the port side. Ham gave Alan a hug. He said, "Be safe and come home in September." Facing the boat, Ham descended down the ladder and then looked up and waved. He saw the old mate and his young man wave back. Ham then retraced his steps to the large door, looked back for a moment, and slipped into the massive monolith.

Ham found his way to the car and drove toward home alone.

It struck Alan that he was his own person. First impressions were important. He was going to do his best and work hard for the great pay and food. "Well, Mr. Briggs, I am ready to go to work."

Briggs said, "First things first. Let's get you signed in." They walked up the filthy ore-cluttered decks of the port side and then crossed the main deck and entered a similar door as on the port side. This time, they went up a set of steel stairs and into a hall, where they found the first mate's quarters.

Briggs asked, "Do you want your pay at the end of the summer in one lump sum or take your pay in weekly checks or cash?" Briggs added, "You don't have anything to spend it on anyway."

Alan remembered Rap's advice and took the mate's word urging. Alan indicated he would wait to the end of the summer to get paid. He completed the pay information necessary to be an employee.

"You're all set, Alan," indicated Briggs.

As they left Briggs's cabin, Alan could feel the boat shift. They were underway. The process was slow as they maneuvered out of the dock in reverse. The crew used the winches and lines attached to spars to move the massive boat. Then there was a right-angle turn, where the freighter was pulled around the corner again through the use of lines attached to a spar. The forward end of boat was pulled back toward the dock as the aft end swung out. When completed, the final deckhand was pulled up to the main deck by hand on a bosun's chair attached to a pendent. The other deckhand and a deck watch did the heavy lifting.

When the boat's lines were free, the coal-fired engines of the fifty-two-year-old boat powerfully moved her out of the slip. The freighter was then turned outward into Lake Michigan.

As the sparkling lights of Chicago glittered and the sun fully set on the western horizon of the water, Alan knew he was on his own. The breeze was fresh and cool.

Alan was excited, nervous, and a bit melancholy for home. He knew Ham would be home in about four more hours.

CHAPTER 16

MEETING THE CREW

"Hey, new guy, come over here!" the watchman yelled.

Alan emerged from below decks where he changed into a sweatshirt and he wore his brand-new work boots. The decks were busy with cleanup and closing activities. The crew on deck consisted of the other two deckhands and the shift deck watch and watchman. The bosun mate was watching the others work. The watchman seemed to be leading the effort.

"Hey, new guy, come over here!" the watchman yelled. "I want you to help latch the line to the hatch covers." He was pointing to the line as one of the deckhands was hooking it to an eye on the heavy plate of steel. Once latched, the deckhand stepped to the other side of the hatch. The winch was engaged, and the line was reeled in through a system of right angles, pulling the hatch cover to closure at the edge of the walkway. The covers were assembled from heavy sliding plates interconnected for pulling the entire assembly. The noise of the winch and sliding steel was deafening.

Alan began to mimic the other workers, and he had the strength to pull the line safely and quickly with one arm. There were thirty-four hatches, and each side needed to be closed as a separate activity. The distance between hatches was about eighteen inches. Due to the slope of the hatches to shed water, the distance from the hatch top to the deck was two to three feet.

Once the hatches were closed, an angle iron about three feet long secured them. The steel device stretched between two hatches. The steel angle had a hole through the center with rod running through it. There was a hook on the bottom end of the rod and the top end was threaded with a butterfly nut. The rod was placed through an eye on the deck and turned tight to secure the hatch covers. There were six of these per hatch cover set.

Upon completion of the hatch cover closing, a wash down of the deck was accomplished, along with setting the light standards in place and plugging them in. The deckhands didn't handle the hose, but the deck watch held the hose and kept it untangled while the watchman directed the jet steam to clear the ore from between each hatch and off the sides into the water.

Alan hadn't been introduced to anyone yet. He simply worked as hard as the other crew members. They finished their work in a couple of hours, including putting away their tools. The crew didn't wear any safety equipment in performing these tasks other than gloves. They certainly didn't wear life vests. The boat was constantly moving beneath their feet. Alan was uneasy at every turn.

As they finished up, the bosun disappeared, but the watchman came over to Alan and held out his hand. "I am Hans." The man was about six feet tall, a bit overweight, and had a vandyked mustache and beard. He looked to be in his forties with a hint of gray in his beard and thinning hair.

Alan shook his hand and said, "I am Alan. Where you from?"

Hans said, "I'm from Minnesota. Yes, I have Swedish heritage, and some call me the Swede."

The deck watch came up and put his hand out. "I'm Frankie." This man was barely five feet six and was scrawny with an unkempt beard. He was a bit younger than Hans, but he was not as polished and had some difficulty looking Alan in the eye.

Alan said, "Hi."

Frankie said, "I'm from Wisconsin."

Then the two deckhands approached Alan. The first said, "I'm Bud." The other said, "I'm Cal." The two were different from each other. Bud was at least five feet ten and had dark hair like Alan. He wore it long and was clean-shaven. He had dark blue eyes and was soft-spoken. Cal was maybe five feet, eight inches with short blond hair and a mustache. He had dark eyes, and his voice was hoarse and crackled when he spoke.

Cal said, "You get the top bunk. I had it until now. You are the new guy."

Bud said, "Is that cool for you?

Alan said, "Sure."

Cal explained, "We are both from Ohio, near Cleveland."

The Swede decided we should all get something to eat. Alan's trip to the galley was memorable. He hadn't eaten since the stop in Kalamazoo many hours earlier. There was no prepared meal at 2200 hours, but the cooler was open, and they made sandwiches. They had water and coffee to drink. These were followed by great bowls of ice cream.

After they meal and a brief moment of storytelling from the day's events, they all went back to their bunks and went to sleep. Alan slept in his clothes. He still felt the boat movement, but it was not as nagging.

The next morning came quickly with the bosun mate rousting the deckhands. "Up and at 'em!" he yelled. "It is seven hundred hours, and we need to be in the galley in ten minutes."

The three deckhands got up, washed in the sink next to the bunk room, and Alan brushed his teeth. They rushed up the stairs and into the bright sunlight. The day was glorious. The sky was filled with wispy clouds, and the water was a brilliant dark blue. The waves were rolling with a light chop at times. The boat was underway with a hint of movement from the sway of the deck.

As Alan made his way to the aft galley, he felt a breeze from the bow. He felt good and well rested. He didn't notice the boat movement at all.

As they entered the galley, the cook, his assistant, and one of the two stewards were busy at the stove and the tables. The other steward served the mates in the dining room. The small tables were stainless steel as was much of the equipment in the galley.

"Hello, I'm Bobby, the cook, and this is my crew." The cook selected his crew for the season, and they were all from Georgia. "This is my assistant and wife, Rosie. This is one of my stewards, Rickie, and Tommie is busy with the captain and mates." They crew was the traditionally black group. They were very polite, soft-spoken, and kind.

"What'll ya have?" Bobby asked.

Alan asked shyly, "What are the choices?" Bobby laughed as did everyone in the galley.

"You ask, and I will make it," Bobby explained.

Alan said, "Bacon and eggs over hard, with toast."

"Coming right up!" Bobby retorted.

The galley was full of deckhands, the bosun mate, and the same deck watch and watchman. Everyone was in good spirits, except for the bosun.

"Hi, I'm Alan," he said softly to the bosun. Everyone noticed the address, and they looked like they were waiting of the response.

The bosun shrugged. He wasn't going to respond but added, "I'm the bosun, but you can call me Hard Rock." He looked Alan right in the eye, as if to say, "I know you have heard of me and I am your worst nightmare."

As they finished eating, Hard Rock said, "Let's get at it."

Rosie said, "Have a great morning" as the crew left the galley.

"Alan, you do what I say, and you will be safe," Hard Rock said flatly, like he had said it a thousand times before. The bosun was short and stocky, but fit.

"We are painting the communications tower today," Hard Rock said gruffly. "Alan, you will do all the climbing. Cal and Bud, you will hand up the tools. Sounds fair?" Everyone agreed.

Up the stairs to the top of the wheelhouse they went. The paint, brushes, sandpaper, rope, and a scrapper were in tow from the paint locker near the deckhands' bunk room.

Hard Rock said, "We can start at the bottom of the tower cleaning and scrapping and work our way up. Then we can paint as we work our way back down."

Alan scrapped and sanded until he reached the top of the tower. He needed little to no help as he worked. He also didn't wear any safety gear and was not tied off to anything. The other three mainly watched him work. The tower was maybe twenty feet high. Add that to the wheelhouse and mate's decks of maybe another thirty feet. Finally, the boat was empty, and the distance from the main deck to the water below was another fifty feet. At over a hundred feet, if Allen fell and didn't hit anything on the way down, he would surely be knocked out by the water and unable to swim.

The water in Lake Michigan was a frigid forty to fifty degrees. If he didn't get pulled in by the slipstream next to the boat and through the two gigantic propellers being chopped to bits, he would die because, with or without a life vest, he couldn't swim in the cold water long enough to wait for the massive boat to slowly turn around before hypothermia would take his life in maybe just less than a half hour.

Occasionally, Hard Rock would yell, "Hey, you missed a spot! Can't you see what you are doing? You are a dumb piece of crap!"

The wind was blowing hard as the bow was pointed into it. Alan hung on tight with one hand and worked with the other hand. Alan remembered his high school coaches saying, "Take care of yourself physically. It will serve you well no matter what to do for a living." This was so true at this moment. He couldn't imagine how hard it would be to climb, work, and hold on if he wasn't in good physical shape.

He also knew that taking care of himself emotionally was also serving him well. He had been trained with an expectation by Ham to have a hard exterior while holding his thoughts and emotions in. Therefore, he could handle a tirade by a person of authority and not break. Alan knew it was better to hold his tongue than to invite an increasingly more aggressive reaction by the bosun mate.

When Alan finished the scrapping, he came down; he needed a bathroom break. Hard Rock immediately got into his face and screamed, "I didn't tell you to come down! I told you we were going to hand the tools up to you. Now get back up there!"

When things seem unreasonable, they are. If Alan wasn't a rookie, he might have been more current with the painting technique of silver paint and the reason the bosun was so pushy. The paint is thin and needs to cover the steel before the air and water adhere to the tower. The faster the paint is applied, the more likely it will adhere. Of course, none of the three deckhands were aware of this. The bosun should have explained himself, but he was in a rage.

Alan needed to advocate his position, but without painting knowledge, he didn't have a chance to push back. Being current is something Alan needed to work on, and it would serve him well as time passed. Advocation was something he needed to practice every day going forward.

Cal said, "It's almost lunchtime. Maybe we could simply pick it up after we eat."

"Hell no!" an agitated Hard Rock yelled. "Back up there, dammit! Now, Alan!"

Alan was shaken, but not showing it, and climbed the tower. Cal and Bud lashed rope to the paint bucket and put the brushes inside. Alan began to paint the very thin, liquid-like silver paint. It sprayed everywhere.

Hard Rock yelled, "Watch out!" Every move Alan made from then on was wrong. He began to take very small amounts of paint on the brush and dapped the tower steel. It worked, but then he was taking too long.

"Hurry up! What are you afraid of?" Hard Rock kept pushing. The galley was ready for them, but Hard Rock wasn't ready for the crew to eat.

"Cal and Bud, you go on ahead. Alan and I will be along shortly," Hard Rock insisted. The two left, clearly happy to be away from the bosun for a least awhile.

"Alan, come down now!" ordered Hard Rock. "You do what I say when I tell you to." Hard Rock looked wild-eyed. His demeanor had become intense. "Yes, I am the soldier and officer your father knew in the South Pacific. I have controlled this poor soul ever since I was killed in the Philippines. I didn't care much for your dad, and I don't care much for you either! Now go to eat."

Alan was shaken to his core. "How could this be?" he said to himself.

CHAPTER 17

CAPTAIN BRADS' VISIT

*"Let me show you a bit more of our
boat, said the captain."*

That afternoon the crew went back to work, and Alan finished his painting. He survived, and the other deckhands did most of the cleanup for the day. Hard Rock didn't change his tact all day. He was brutal, and the tongue-lashings were unyielding.

As they were passing by the wheelhouse, Captain Brads waved to the crew. They all stopped, but Brads said, "Just you, Alan." The others left, and Alan stayed behind. Brads said, "I worked with your grandfather for many years, even on this boat. I was his third mate at one time. He was a great seaman. He knew everything and had been through a lot from a shipwreck to Coast Guard officer during the World War II. He sailed the entire fleet and was well respected by everyone.

"Let me show you a bit more of our boat," said the captain. They climbed the stairs. "This, of course, is the wheelhouse." It was large and spanned the entire width of the boat. There were instruments and, of course, a large center wheel to steer the boat.

The windows give a glorious view of where we were heading and where we had been. "We can see about ten miles in either direction even with the curvature of Earth," explained Brads.

Alan was introduced to the second mate, the wheelsman, deck watch, and watchman. Alan already had met the Swede and Frankie, but everyone acted like the captain was doing the honors of first-time introductions.

The captain then took Alan to the aft of the boat. They went down to the engine room, where the temperature rose by twenty degrees. It was a hot, noisy place where a licensed engineer, operator or oiler, and a wiper were on shift. Alan thought to himself how lucky he was to be a deckhand and not a wiper. They didn't stay long and went up to the main deck but, this time, went around the back of the bulkhead, past the port side lifeboat, and looked out to a view of where they had been. The wave train seemed to go on for a mile or more. It was a beautiful white strip on a sea of brilliant blue.

They strode to a closed door, and the captain opened it. It was the dining room for the officers of the boat. It was well-appointed with white linens and china. Brads said, "Well, this is where I say good evening." He shut the door behind him. It was clear that status and rank were evident and that it meant something real to the captain.

Alan went back around to the galley and joined in for the evening meal. It was an interesting day, but a bit scary physically and emotionally. They had one-pound hamburgers with huge home-cut fries. Alan had two burgers and several glasses of milk. They all had cherry pie with ice cream for dessert.

After dinner, Alan joined a couple of others in the library, where they played cards in the aft cabins between the galley and the chief engineer's cabin. Alan enjoyed the difficulty of the game of hearts that they played. He was good at it and won a couple of games. He didn't stay long and headed back to the bunk room.

He cleaned up and went to bed. However, Alan worried about the bosun across the deck in his cabin.

• • • • • • • • • • ● • • • • • • • • • •

CHAPTER 18

UNDER THE BRIDGE AND THROUGH THE LOCKS

"Now the water is deadly scary," exclaimed Alan.

"Get up!" yelled Hard Rock. "We are going to go through the Soo Locks this morning."

Alan made it to the deck by the time they were just going under the Mighty Mac Bridge. The Mackinaw Bridge was opened in 1957 and was just about five miles long. It was about five hundred feet off the water, and as they went under the span, it seemed almost unbelievable that it could hold itself erect, let alone a string of automobiles.

They crew had breakfast, and Hard Rock continued to be sullen and disagreeable. His eyes continued to be intense. Hard Rock said, "Alan, you and me again today."

Cal said, "He needed to do something, and he would catch up with us in a bit."

As Alan and Bud prepared the gear to go through the locks, Cal went toward the captain's quarters. He entered and said, "Hi, Dad."

Brads said cheerfully, "Hello. What's up, son?"

Cal stated, "I know Bud and Sis are getting married in a few weeks. I haven't had time to get prepared with a present for them or get measured for my tuxedo."

Brads said, "Me either. I know your mother is concerned about the logistics. I don't want you to worry, and Mom said she will measure your tux from the suit you wore to high school graduation."

Cal questioned, "I don't know about that. I am bigger now."

Brads curtly quipped, "Stop. Mom said she would take care of it. Now go!"

Cal was angry and hurt. He wanted to be included in the plans for the first wedding of a family member in his lifetime.

They made it to the locks through the St. Marys River. With the boat being empty, the Alan and Bud were let off the short height to dock side by bosun's chair.

A bosun's chair is a flat board with a hole in the middle. A rope is fed through the board, and a knot is tied using the short end. The long end of rope is then fed through a pulley such that someone can to swing out from the deck. The line is held by a couple of men. The crew member on the chair has the rope between his legs and can hang on to the rope for balance as it is raised or lowered by pulling in the rope or letting it out. Of course, tension is kept on the line to ensure no quick or jerky action is felt by the crew member on the bosun's chair.

Hard Rock and Cal manned the rope and let both deckhands down. Bud was first, and the careful lowering seemed well-done compared to the jerky ride down that Hard Rock provided to Alan.

Taglines of a smaller-size rope are attached to the large steel cable eyes by using a knot that can be easily untied with one hand. The bowline is the knot of choice. Then the lines are pulled until the steel lines are ashore. These cables are then pulled by one deckhand to a spar to moor the boat to the lock's side. As water is let into the lock from Lake Superior, the boat rises to the level of upper lake. Then the lines are released, and deckhands are pulled up once again to the boat's deck. Then the boat moved out toward the open lake waters. All this was accomplished by the crew through midafternoon.

After lunch, the crew simply made themselves busy for the next day's work. Hard Rock pulled Alan aside and said, "Don't you ever let me see you walking around with Captain Brads again. You need to know your place and not get hurt." Alan was horrified.

The deckhands ate dinner and went back to the cabin together. As they walked along the deck, Alan looked out at the black waters of Lake Superior. He could see a million stars in the sky.

Alan explained out loud, "I have never seen the sky like this before. There are so many stars out there. Much more than I thought. I just have never seen the sky so brilliant, and I didn't know what I was missing."

Bud said, "Yeah, it is amazing."

"Now the water is deadly scary," exclaimed Alan.

Cal said, "You wouldn't want to fall in. You would surely die. The boat could turn around, but at night, it would be impossible to find you out there all alone without a light."

They all agreed, but it all seemed a little divergent. The stars had a brilliance that was unreal and out of reach. The water had an opaqueness that seemed very close and urgent.

When they reached the cabin, they simply sat around and talked.

Alan said, "I have enjoyed my first trip. The work is varied, and I must say easy enough. I have worked harder for my dad."

Bud agreed tacitly. Cal, on the other hand, was clearly upset.

"I am not enjoying the work. I am not happy with the officers of the boat. I am not happy," Cal blurted out. "I just wish that there was more time in port to go off and have some fun."

Bud said, "We don't have any money anyway. What kind of fun could we have?"

Cal stated flatly, "Maybe I could do something that didn't cost any money."

Alan said, "I'm eighteen, and I'm not going out to any club or bars. I am okay with what is happening, except for one thing. I think Hard Rock has it out for me."

"Who are you talking about?" asked Cal.

"You know, the bosun mate," retorted Alan.

Cal stated flatly, "His name is Robert. He told you that the first day in the galley."

Alan said, "I heard Hard Rock."

Bud said, "Sorry, Alan, he said Robert. You misheard."

"Okay, but he made me do the entire tower the first day," Alan pleaded.

Bud said, "That was your initiation, I think. We all have been through something like it, but maybe with a little less anger. It is to see if you can handle the work without any help from us."

Alan said as he was feeling ashamed, "He held me back and made me go up the tower as you went to lunch. I had to work while you were in the galley."

Finally, Cal said, "C'mon. He gave you an order, you were supposed to follow it. I think you should lighten up a bit."

Bud said wistfully, "It been a long day, and we aren't having a good time talking about you and bosun."

The three went to bed and said good night in turn. Cal was last.

Cal seemed despondent but managed to say, "Good night."

· · · · · · · · · ● · · · · · · · · ·

CHAPTER 19

NORTHERN LIGHTS

*Alan couldn't believe his eyes. There in
the sky was a moving mass of light.*

The Swede came into the deckhand bunk room. He turned on the lights like he owned the room. "Hey, you guys want to see the northern lights?"

Bud said, "No."

Cal said, "No, I've already seen them. Now turn out the lights."

Alan said, "Sure, what are they?"

The Swede said, "C'mon."

Alan jumped down from his upper bunk, pulled on his jeans, and went out the door.

The Swede said, "C'mon, but go back and turn out the lights. Are you inconsiderate at all hours of the day and night?"

They both laughed as they bounded up the steel-treaded stairs.

The Swede explained as they went out on deck and into the darkness of the night, "The northern lights are called officially aurora borealis, and they are the most fantastic light show provided to us by Mother Nature."

"Okay," continued the watchman. "It's two in the morning. The skies are clear and no moon. It is dark out here, and there won't be any ambient light to block out the light show."

"We will see a sky full of stars. But we will also see lights that demonstrate both physics and chemistry. The light flares are particles with an electrical charge from the sun, interacting with our Earth's atmosphere. The colors are from element interaction with nitrogen giving the sky a red, violet, and at times, a blue hue. Particles colliding with oxygen give off a yellow and green glow. Other elements give off pink, orange, and white colors."

The two men moved toward the midsection of the boat. The Swede pulled the plug on the deck lights at the edge of the hull. The night was dark, and with no ambient light, the sky was spectacular. There was a myriad of stars. The two took up positions on adjacent hold hatch covers and lay down. With this vantage point, the stars were simply everywhere.

Alan began to recognize the Big and Little Dipper. He also could see the North Star and the constellation Orion. He recognized that he clearly didn't know much about what he was looking at. In the city, even a small one like Alan's home, you simply can't see many stars due to the light of the homes, buildings, and even streetlights. He didn't know what he was missing.

The Milky Way, Alan deduced, was the massive spiral cluster of stars he could see. Our solar system is situated within it, and our sun orbits around the center of the galaxy. To have scientists begin to determine how the universe works and to have additional information from satellites, such as the data from going to the moon, makes this time exciting.

Alan yelled, "Hey, where's the light show?"

The Swede exclaimed, "Isn't all this enough?"

Alan rolled over on his side, and with arm bent at the elbow, he placed his head on his hand. "Okay, yes!" he declared. "But I was hoping for more."

The Swede said, "Sit up and face the north."

Alan said, "Which way?"

The Swede was now fixated on the horizon. "Look straight out on the starboard side of the boat. Look right out there." He pointed to the sky.

Alan couldn't believe his eyes. There in the sky was a moving mass of light. It was green with waves of light coming into view. The dancing of the green haze seemed to be surreal. It appeared to be ghostlike or a haze from some ghastly movie. Then the colors deepened, and they saw a curtain of red above the dark green shimmer.

The show was the most beautiful natural phenomenon Alan had ever seen. The lights seemed to exist for just these two men on this particular summer's night. Of course, the show has been a constant activity for eons between the sun and its satellite, Earth. The men just happened to be in the right place on the right night.

The Swede said, "It's going to be dawn soon. We better get to bed."

Alan thanked his guide for the evening for the great show and enlightening education.

The Swede didn't have to ask the deckhands to come to the deck that night. The Swede knew the light show would occur due to his experience and the fact the conditions were quite right.

Alan took him up on the offer and recognized how generous it was. The other two deckhands simply missed the opportunity to see the show but, more importantly, to gain a deeper understanding of the Swede as a mentor. Mentoring helps.

Alan returned to his bunk. The other two deckhands both grunted an annoying, "Thanks for waking me up again."

Everyone was asleep in moments.

CHAPTER 20

WORK AND MAKING PORT

*Hard Rock picked at Alan. Alan didn't
work fast enough, or he wasn't careful.*

The deckhands heard the bosun yell, "Get up! Let's get to breakfast and then to work!"

Up they hurried and out on deck they went. It was overcast and cold. It didn't take long for the crew to be assembled for breakfast. Bobby and Rosie declared at almost the same time, "Good morning, boys."

"What'll you have?" Bobby inquired.

They placed their orders and told stories. Frankie said, "Okay, Alan, what is the difference between a fairy tale and a story the Swede tells?"

Alan thought better than to answer and said, "I don't know."

Frankie delightedly said, "A fairy tale starts out, 'Once upon a time,' but the Swede's story begins, 'This is no crap.' They both have the same amount of truth."

Everyone laughed.

The food came quickly, and it was devoured just as fast. Out the door they exploded and across the deck to the tool room they proceeded. The crew was still laughing, and the mood was good.

The bosun pulled Alan aside. "I am Hard Rock. I will work you as I see fit. No complaint?" he asked.

"Are you Rob...?" Alan started.

"Shut up. I am Hard Rock. Watch yourself," was the response. His eyes were glaring.

"Okay," Alan gave in.

The crew worked with grinders and mechanical scrappers all day. They didn't wear hearing protection, except for the Swede. He wore earmuffs, but it wasn't clear that the gear was helpful or if he was just warming his ears. The day was cold and windy. Therefore, the work itself was useful to keep warm.

Hard Rock picked at Alan. Alan didn't work fast enough, or he wasn't careful. Alan had to go get the tools for himself and others when needed. Alan worked on the largest section of deck, cleaned the old paint away and swept up the old debris, and threw it overboard.

Hard Rock screamed at Alan, "Throw that crap off the port side, not the starboard side! That way, the debris doesn't blow back on board! You don't spit into the wind, do you?" Alan did as commanded. But the crap blew back on board. Then Alan had to clean the deck of the debris again as Hard Rock weighed in. Alan then threw the dirt overboard on the starboard side to Hard Rock's chagrin. Nothing came back, except Hard Rock's anger.

"I told you the port side," yelled Hard Rock. The crew looked bewildered as they were dismissed for lunch. "Alan, do what I want, or you will get hurt!" Alan was dismissed for lunch, and Hard Rock went another way around the corner.

After a lunch of cheeseburgers the size of the large pancakes and with country fries, they all went back to work. The afternoon process was repeated with Alan taking the brunt of the load. The afternoon was full of painting and then putting the tools away.

The crew ate and were told to go to bed early. The port of Duluth, Minnesota, was going to make the early morning an adventure. On the way to the crew quarters, Cal stayed behind as he saw Rosie coming out of the captain's cabin. He didn't trust his dad and wondered what she was up to.

The crew went to bed.

"Up. Now!" the bosun summoned. Up and out into the early-morning light they went. The Duluth break wall had been made by the *Demson*, and the water was calm. The city lights were glowing on the hillside, and the docks were at the end of the wall. As they approached the shoreline, Alan saw extremely large cranes in place and all set to load iron ore into the three hulls of their freighter.

As the deckhands worked to winch open the hatches with the deck watch and watchman, they drew ever closer to the docks of Duluth. Once near enough, the deckhands were lowered by bosun chair and pulled the taglines and then the attached steel cables to the spars out forward and aft of the boat. When completed the deckhands would take turns on the lines in case they needed to be moved. When relieved, the deckhands would eat and go to the bathroom.

When Cal was released, he went into the galley. Rosie was there. "Hi, Cal, what'll have?" said Bobby.

Cal said, "Bacon and eggs over easy with toast."

"Coming right up," was the joyous answer from Bobby.

Cal waved Rosie over. "Did you see my dad yesterday?" inquired Cal.

"Yes, a couple of times," Rosie said with a question on her face.

Cal said, "Don't be that way. Did you go to my father's cabin? Yes or no."

Rosie said, "Yes, after dinner I think is what you are referring to. He wanted me to repair a shirt for him. He wants to wear it at your sister's wedding. It was torn. I said I would fix it, but it had to be tomorrow as we are in port today."

Cal was ashamed and said, "I am having a rough day. I am sorry."

Cal left the galley and proceeded up the main deck on the port side. Funny but the port side was not at the dock but out toward the harbor. About halfway up the deck, a tender was lashed to the *Demson*. A ladder from the deck down to the fifty-foot-long boat was available for the crew to descend. Cal climbed down and went into the large cabin.

Once Cal was in, it was dark in the cabin with just a few incandescent, bare lightbulbs and the air was a bit musty. The cabin seemed very small compared to its outside appearance.

As Cal's eyes grew accustomed to the diminished light, he looked around. The place was filled with a myriad of treasures. The fare included snack foods and candy, cameras with film and transistor radios, knives, shaving gear, music cassettes, books and magazines, postcards with pens and paper, gloves and hats, sun and magnifying glasses, fishing line and lures, and cheap trinkets and peculiar junk. Cal walked around, didn't buy anything, and left.

Cal said under his breath, "I wouldn't want to touch anything in there. I might catch something."

Cal's break was over.

The loading went without a hitch, and the boat was loaded in about eight hours. When the lines were released, the deckhands were lifted back on board. The closing operation took place and the wash down and replacing the lighting standards began. As they cleared the break wall, the boat was secured tightly as it was a normal safety routine.

Alan retrieved a book on black history from the library. He read the first several chapters before going to bed.

CHAPTER 21

ANOTHER SAIL AND AN AWAKENING

Alan said, "Bobby is a man."

The next day started with a similar routine as the others. Get up, eat breakfast, and organize for a work detail. The day was crisp, windy, and cloud covered. It was refreshing.

The bosun said, "We are right back on the aft deck scrapping this morning. I would like everyone to work continuously so we can clear the deck by the time the captain has lunch. No groaning!"

The crew worked hard and finished the scrapping and cleanup before the morning was through. They finished just as the captain and mates began to walk around the corner.

"Hi, men," said the captain.

"Hello," the crew mumbled.

"Looks like you have been working hard," the captain professed. "Alan, good to see you. It looks like you fit right in. C'mon, mates, let's see what Bobby has prepared for us. He is a good boy."

Alan knew that this was demeaning. He couldn't put his finger on it, but the cook's crew seemed to be a considered a bit lower in status than everyone else on the boat. In comparison to the cook's and steward's role, it seemed like everyone else's role was considered a little better by the crew. It seemed like it made everyone other than the cook's crew feel good about themselves.

The crew was black, and they were from the South, where as everyone else on board was white and from the North. The word *boy* is pejorative. Everyone perceived that the nature of the role was the nature of the person filling the role. The cook, stewards, and all blacks had the same station in life. This is exactly what everyone thought that was standing there. No big deal?

Alan knew differently. He grew up in an elementary school with black students. His best friend was Hispanic. He had teachers that were black. The condition of a person is not due to the color of his skin unless someone is working this issue against him.

Alan said, "Bobby is a man."

Hard Rock immediately took Alan's arm so tightly that it hurt and pulled him away and around the bulkhead. "I told you to stay away from the captain," Hard Rock admonished. "What might be true is not always what is said. Now lock your jaw!"

Cal, still back with the captain, said, "He didn't mean anything by what he said. He is just a kid and naive. The bosun will straighten him out."

Brads declared, "It's okay. Now, Cal, shut up!"

Cal was seething mad. He was called out again by his dad and, this time, in front of the crew. He was considered a "boy" by his dad. He didn't like it. No, he wasn't happy.

Alan thought that everyone has the right to be heard. Cal should be able to at least voice his opinion. The rule of captain first and the crew second certainly didn't work for Cal, the captain's son. He should be allowed to ask for a change in the dialogue between them in a civilized manner.

The idea of raising a question to a superior should not be a scary or unwelcomed event or activity. This is how better decisions are made. This is how change for the better occurs. It should be allowed. It should be welcomed by anybody, especially your son.

Hard Rock was ornery, but the afternoon's work was completed without incident. Cal and Bud seemed to have angry words during the day. Still not knowing anything about the relationship Cal or Bud had with the captain, Alan was completely oblivious.

Alan continued to read the black history book after dinner. He was becoming aware of the fact that just because someone has a position of authority, they are not morally right on every area of life. This is a good area of discovery for Alan because he should know when it is okay to disagree with the boss or, better yet, the boss's boss?

Cal and Bud continued their discussion. Cal asked, "When are you going to get measured for your tux?"

Bud replied, "I don't know, but your dad said it would happen in time for the tailor to complete his work before the wedding."

Cal said, "The wedding is in three weeks. I would think it would be soon. What if we don't go to Lake Huron and down to Lake Erie on this trip? There will be no time."

Bud said, "Look, trust your parents! Now get off it. It is a sore subject."

Cal said, "Okay. I'm sorry. I just want things to go well."

Alan came in the bunk room. He said, "Hi. I am tired. I'm going to sleep."

Two deckhands went to sleep, but Cal kept thinking about the wedding and his dad's respect.

CHAPTER 22

THE SOO AND LAKE HURON

*A disgruntled Hard Rock spit, "I didn't want to be
in this rain for this long. Get used to the cold water.
You will need to understand how it feels sometime."*

The crew was rousted very early to move the boat through the locks. It was windy, and it felt like the temperature was near freezing. As they did their work, Alan could hear birds waking up for their day. Lights were on, but they weren't quite needed anymore. The boat made it through to the lower level of the river, and the crew was off to breakfast.

The watchman was at the bow of the boat to look for hazards and watch out for other boats in the right of way while in the river. This morning was foggy but would become clear as the day wore on. For now, the foghorn blew every minute from within the deep steam vibrating steel plates—high note followed by low note.

The decision by dispatch was for the *Demson* to go to Conneaut, Ohio, by way of Lake Huron, the St. Clair River, Lake St. Clair, the Detroit River, and finally, Lake Erie.

The day was, again, a day of work. Painting was the chore and completion of the back deck by the captain's dining room was the location.

Hard Rock said sternly, "We must get done with the chipping by lunchtime."

Cal and Bud chimed in, "So we are out of the way for the captain and the other officers to make their way to eat."

Hard Rock looked at them and then at Alan, who hadn't said a thing. Hard Rock said, "Alan, keep your mouth shut."

The work was hard, and the weather was overcast. By midmorning, it began to rain, a cold steady rain. The back deck was a mess with paint chip and debris. Hard Rock told Bud and Cal to begin to pick up the tools. He told Alan to finish the section he was chipping. The tools the other two were using were put away quickly, and they were told to go to the library around the corner. Alan was told to finish. He worked through the rain and wind. Finally, the chipping was finished. Only then he was berated by Hard Rock for not being quicker.

A disgruntled Hard Rock spit, "I didn't want to be in this rain for this long. Get used to the cold water. You will need to understand how it feels sometime."

The captain was coming. Alan had to clean up the debris and the tools. He didn't quite get done in time. The captain made the corner and stopped in his tracks.

"What is this mess? I don't want to walk through the chips and dirt," declared Brads angrily.

Hard Rock said that Alan had been working slowly due to the rain. "I will go get the other two to help."

Brads said, "No, this is Alan's problem and he can fix it. I will slip into the chief engineer's cabin for a minute while the simple-minded deckhand of a boy finishes his work!"

Alan worked even harder yet to sweep the dirt up and put it overboard. He picked up his tools and took them to the locker. He met the other deckhands in the galley, where they were almost finished.

Bud said, "What happened to you?"

Alan, almost in tears, explained, "I had to finish the entire section in the rain. I didn't get done in time for the captain to come to eat. He saw I wasn't finished, scolded me, and retreated to the chief's cabin."

Cal said, "Let me see if I get this. You finished our work and got in trouble for not being quicker, all in the rain? That's nuts!"

Bud asked, "Where's the bosun when all this happened?"

Alan said as the bosun walked in, "He was there."

Hard Rock said to Alan, "The captain's now eating in the dining room. He wasn't happy, but I explained that you were doing extra duty. I told you from the beginning that I didn't want the captain to see or hear you again."

Alan asked, "Why was I doing extra duty? Why was I working in the rain?"

Hard Rock snarled, "We work in the rain all the time. You are getting paid to work and to follow orders!"

Alan asked, "What about the others?"

Hard Rock yelled, "I am your bosun and you do what I say. Period!"

The captain stuck his head in the galley. "Alan, come to see me after lunch. It looks like a rain out anyway."

Hard Rock was livid. This was his deckhand, and the captain was interfering. "Captain Brads, I can handle Alan. Just leave it to me."

Brads said, "No."

Alan cleaned his plate. He got up to go.

Hard Rock said, "I am done with you! I just want you to be safe. I can't help you right now."

They walked together toward the forward part of the boat. Then Hard Rock disappeared down the stairway.

Alan was shaking. He went up to the captain's cabin and knocked.

Brads said, "I like your ability to work hard. I am not upset with you. I think Robert has been a bit hard on you, especially as your first bosun mate. Fairness is important. I respect Bobby, and I am sorry you took my comments wrong. He is special to me and has been working with me since he was eighteen. I think of him as my boy or son. Are we okay?"

Alan was relieved. "Yes, sir."

Brads said, "Okay. Now go back to the crew."

The crew was in the library. The bosun was nowhere to be found. The crew spent the afternoon telling stories and practicing making knots.

This was a lesson in how not to teach someone a physical activity.

Frankie said, "Okay, let me tell you how to make a half hitch. Then I show you myself."

They started watching Frankie first describe what a half hitch knot was. "It is created by bringing the rope over and then under this standing table leg." He then took the rope and flipped it around the leg, and when he took his hands away, it might as well have been a magic trick. No one saw what he did, but everyone saw the outcome.

With some protesting from the deckhands, he went onto the figure-eight knot. Frankie said, "Look, this one is just as easy. The tail of the rope is looped over itself and then the end is put under itself and back through the loop." He had both hands working. The knot was made in slow motion, but after he was done and passed it around, no one could duplicate the feat.

Frankie, a bit exasperated with all the students, declared, "This is the best of all, the versatile bowline knot. We use this knot all the time. If you remember one knot, this is one. A small loop is made at the end of the rope, leaving enough for the desired size of the eventual loop. The tail is passed through the loop, under and then over the end, and finally back through the loop to complete. We say the rabbit came out of the hole around the tree and then back into the hole again." Frankie was really good at it. He showed us several times, but no one mastered it.

Frankie said, "It'll take practice for you to get good."

What he didn't realize is that if he really wanted to teach the deckhands this physical activity, he should have put the rope in their hands and talked them through it multiple times until they got it.

Alan learned a lot that day about dreams lost, women and lost hope of the men, and the dreary life of their repetitive ore trips year after year. He also learned a lot about knot making where none if makes any sense unless you have the rope in your hands while the master coaches. The Socratic method would be helpful with open-ended questions and guidance.

All the while during the afternoon, the Swede didn't join in the rope tying, but he did join the conversations while he was working on a piece of soft wood with his knife. The piece was one inch square and about a foot long. He was making a wooden chain without breaks in any link. Alan was in awe.

Later, they all went to dinner together. The food was great. There were hamburgers that were six inches in diameter with home-made fries. There was rhubarb pie with ice cream for dessert. After eating, they played card games, including euchre and hearts. No one gambled.

After an enjoyable evening, they went to bed.

• • • • • • • • • ● • • • • • • • • •

CHAPTER 23

THE RIVERS AND LAKE ERIE

Frankie didn't swing back but swore
and said, "It was just a joke."

In the morning, the rain had stopped. Hard Rock yelled, "Get up! This is going to be a tough day. We are going to start with cleaning out the tool locker. Then we're going to finish the main aft deck, and if we have time, we are going to begin the upper aft deck. All the while, the views are going to be spectacular down the river."

"Alan, how did it go with the captain?" Hard Rock inquired.

"It was fine," Alan replied. Alan didn't say anything about the comments the captain made concerning Hard Rock and unfair treatment. He figured it would just set the bosun off.

Hard Rock just looked blankly with wild eyes at Alan and said nothing.

As they approached the galley, there was a commotion. It seems Frankie had taken an orange from the refrigerator and put it in a dish towel. He asked Cal if he wanted to see a peach.

Cal said, "What do you mean?"

Frankie had the orange squeezed in his right hand and the other end of the towel in his left. He pulled the towel taught from his groin. "Ever see such a peach?" Frankie laughed.

Cal would have none of the joke and punched Frankie.

Frankie didn't swing back but swore and said, "It was just a joke."

Cal looked foolish again to everyone. He bolted away and left the galley.

Bobby broke the tension and said, "C'mon in, fellas. What'll have?"

Everyone ordered to their liking. Alan sat with Bud and Swede.

The Swede said, "Frankie has been doing the peach thing for years. It's harmless."

Bud said, "Cal's just having a tough trip and feels picked on. He's the wrong guy to tease right now."

Alan pitched in with, "I think the joke was tasteless, but it was funny."

The food came, they ate, and chitchatted until it was time to go to work.

Distractions are always at hand. Alan thought, *Don't lose focus on what you are doing. The main reason for this job is money for college.* Beyond that, he was building his reputation separate from his family. He was also building his résumé for the future jobs he might apply for. He will have skills and knowledge that should help him in the future.

They weren't far from the southernmost point of Lake Huron, where there is a bridge from the United States to Canada. The lake empties into a river called St. Clair.

Hard Rock stated with a bite, "Let's get going!"

The tool locker had become a mess after the rain of the past day. The tarps were wet. Some of the tools were as well. They completely emptied the tool locker. What Alan found was disturbing.

There was a military rifle and a samurai sword. They both seemed to come from the World War II era. Probably from Southeast Asia based upon the lettering on the weapons. Hard Rock simply walked over and began to clean each item. Alan was flabbergasted! These weapons were completely illegal on board. Hard Rock called Alan over and whispered, "These are the tools we needed to make it through the campaign on Luzon."

The rest of the crew didn't see a rifle or a sword. They saw a crowbar and a mop. The other crew members were not alarmed and said nothing.

Alan replied to Hard Rock, "These are unacceptable on this freighter."

Hard Rock said softly, "These are necessary on the ship heading to New Guinea."

"But we are on our way to Lake Erie," Alan retorted.

Cal shouted at everyone to be quiet. "We are entering the river. Look, Alan, I think that it is your family waving to you from under the bridge on shore."

Alan looked out, and indeed it was Ham and Elm. He hadn't seen either one for a few of weeks. It was good to experience a bit of home even though it was from a distance. Alan waved, and they waved even more wildly. Alan yelled, but they couldn't hear him across the distance and the ambient rushing noise from the current. They continued to wave until the *Demson* was out of sight. It was quick, and it was over. The current was fast as they entered the river. The whole lake was fighting to get into river's banks.

The river is treacherous with curves, shallow spots, and other boats. The river and lakes are dredged to be sure that there is a least thirty-five-foot draft for the boats. The *Demson*, being loaded, needed all that to be safe through the waters. Lake St. Clair was very shallow and the shipping channel was marked, but the watchful eye of the watchmen was very important.

The crew finished its work on the locker. They took the tools they needed to the aft deck and completed the last section of deck by noon. The galley was open, but everyone took their lunch on deck and observed the people doing routine activity. This included people walking their dogs, biking, and driving to wherever they needed to go. The day was cool, but brilliantly sunny. The trip across Lake St. Clair offered a different view of pleasure craft, sunbathers, fishermen, and the passing of another freighter heading up bound.

The crew began working on the upper aft deck as they passed the city of Detroit and, to its south, the city of Windsor, Ontario.

That's right. This is the only place Canada is south of the United States.

As they worked, the sites were interesting, but most of all, the *J. W. Wescott* mail boat came out from the Detroit post office and pulled alongside the *Demson*. A bucket on a rope was let down with mail from the *Demson*. When it came back up, mail for the *Demson* was in the bucket. The mail went to the first mate's office. If there was something for a crew member, it was placed on their bunk. When the deckhands finished their work for the day, they would see if they had received any mail.

· · · · · · · · ● · · · · · · · ·

CHAPTER 24

THE ACCIDENT AND REPAIR

The entire boat was in a two-node sine curve.

The deckhands continued to work through the day and was nearing completion when they felt a thump. They weren't sure of what happened, but it became quite apparent that something bad occurred.

As they looked out from the upper aft deck toward the forward end of the boat, they were shocked at what they saw. The entire boat was in a two-node sine curve. As the bow rose, so did the aft end. Then the bow and aft fell, and the midsection rose. This phenomenon continued seven or eight times a minute.

Alan remembered seeing video of a Washington bridge in physics class that galloped in the same manner hours before it came apart and fell into the river below. The *Demson* frequency, amplitude of maybe ten feet, and the distance from node to node of over hundred feet was clearly textbook. There is a lot of force involved to set up this phenomenon.

The deckhands and most of the shipmates didn't know what happened, but something rough must have occurred. Upon inspection, the wheelsman got out of the shipping channel and one of the rotor blades on one of the two propellers was broken off. This set up a harmonic rhythm, and boat began to move to the wave period. Scientists and engineers call it galloping.

The boat was slowed. Carefully and tediously, the *Demson* made its way to Toledo, Ohio, for further instruction from the Steel Company officials.

Cal was very anxious due to the plans that were needed to be made for the wedding. He wanted to talk to his mother, and he wanted off the boat. He went to his father. "Dad, let me go home. Mom can come to pick me up from Cleveland if we get there."

Brads said, "That's the point. Cal, I have plenty to worry about with the seaworthiness of the vessel. I am not sure what is going to happen, and we might not be able to sail for some time."

Cal demanded to be let off the *Demson* and to talk to his mother.

Brads said with anger, "No! No one leaves the boat until we find out what to do. Now go back to your crew."

Cal was devastated.

The deckhands put their tools away. The galley was opened a bit early as everyone was completely confused and worried about what the next action would be. The dinner was veal with baked potato, and the desert was apple pie. It seemed a bit unreflective of the state they were in; nothing seemed as easy as apple pie.

After being in Toledo overnight, the *Demson* was released to go to Cleveland for repair. The trip in Lake Erie was painstakingly slow as to not cause any more vibration-induced sine curves on deck. The deckhands were stationed on deck to observe any vibration from the imbalanced propeller action.

Alan noted that Lake Erie is shallow, and the color of the water went from blue at times to brown and even green with algae. Alan declared, "The lake looks like a large river, but the flow isn't sufficient to clean out all the gunk in the water."

Bud said as they looked out across the water, "The steel mills the *Demson* feeds is one cause of the low quality of the lake water. I know beaches that are contaminated."

Cal pitched in, "I was taught in Ohio history class that the lake was named after the Iroquois Tribe that lived along its shores."

No work was done that travel day. No one wanted anything else to go wrong even if it was a minor injury. The boat arrived by the evening. The deckhands were put on shore and tied up the *Demson*.

The process was to unload the boat and then winch down on the bow of the boat, lifting the screws out of the water. The propeller would be changed out, and the bow of the boat would be let down after. The work should take a couple of days. The investigation into the wheelsman's error would also be made.

Captain Brads told the first mate, Ken Briggs, "Take over the boat's command while the repairs are underway. I am going home to see the family, and I am taking…" Brads hesitated and finished with, "Bud with me."

Briggs said, "Aye, aye, Captain."

Brads gathered a few things and met Bud on the dock. They left before dinner. The captain and Bud were picked up by Cal's mom, Lil, and his sister in their white and grayish-green Chevy Impala. The ride was delightful, and then they had dinner at a family restaurant not far from their home. The next day, the captain and Bud got measured for tuxedos. Cal's mom asked the captain for Cal's measurements for the tux he would wear. Brads said, "I thought he would be able to wear the same size as his high school graduation suit."

Lil shook her head. "He is bigger than he was then. I will just have to guess. Why didn't you bring him along?" Lil obviously knew what had happened because she got a call from Cal from the Cleveland dock.

Brads annoyed said, "I needed two deckhands to handle the lines on board. It was either Bud or Cal. I chose Bud."

Lil said, "That is awful. You shouldn't have to choose someone other than your own son."

Back on board the *Demson*, Cal went to dinner. There was chop suey to eat that evening. But this was after the *Demson* got in port. He saw Alan and asked, "Where is Bud?"

Alan said, "I don't know. Wasn't he with you this afternoon?"

Cal said, "Yes, but I haven't seen him for more than an hour. I thought he was here."

Rosie said, "I think I saw him go somewhere with Captain Brads. When we were getting the supplies for our next trip, I saw him get in a green car with the captain."

Cal was horrified. "What did you say? You saw Bud and my dad getting into my mother's car?"

Alan was shocked. He was just finding out that Cal was the captain's son!

Rosie knew the relationship as did most everyone else on board. Rosie said, "I thought you should know."

Cal stormed out, left the boat, and called home. Of course, no one was home yet because they went out for dinner. But when Cal called again a few hours later, Lil picked up the phone. Cal was sobbing. "Dad left me. I thought I would be able to get measured for my tux and get something for Sis for her wedding. I don't think I will be able to get back again for the wedding tasks I have to complete. Mom, I am bigger than I was when I graduated from high school," he sobbed.

Lil was heartbroken for her son. Lil said, "I know. I'm sorry. I know."

Cal hung up and left the *Demson* dock. He boarded another Steelworks boat and went below decks as a stowaway.

Alan didn't see either deckhand the rest of the time the *Demson* was unloaded and repaired. He did double duty, but Hard Rock didn't bother him either. Alan didn't sleep for the duration of the overhaul and unloading as he was working to perform all deckhand work.

Hard Rock had been let go. He had been drinking. He gathered his things and left without a word to Alan. In addition, Captain Brads didn't like his treatment of the deckhands, especially Alan.

A new bosun came on board but didn't introduce himself as the crew was very busy and needed to concentrate on their tasks at hand.

The process for repair, however, worked very well, and in thirty-seven hours, the entire activity list was done. The investigation was also completed with no fault found. The wheelsman was put on notice that his actions would be monitored, but nothing else. The boat was committed back to service and released to go.

The captain and Bud returned from their breakaway refreshed and accomplished. The difference this time was Lil came with them. She was going to make the round trip. If the timing worked out right, she would be back for the wedding planning with more than a week to spare. Lil wanted the break, and she desperately wanted to see Cal.

Lil knew the captain was away most of the time while the kids were growing up, and the relationship with both was not as easy and natural as most children would have encountered with their father. The summer experience for Cal was supposed to be a bonding opportunity before he went away to college.

Now the fissure between father and son was wide and deep. Lil hoped to salvage something between them.

The *Demson* was readied, and off they went into Lake Erie heading toward Duluth again.

CHAPTER 25

HORROR AND DISAPPOINTMENT

*Neither Alan nor Bud knew where Cal was. Alan
hadn't seen him since the galley discussion with Rosie.*

"Hey, fellas, get up," said the new bosun delightfully.
"Cal, your mom is on board and would like to see
you." He looked at Bud.

"I'm Bud. Who are you?" Bud questioned.

"Oh, I'm sorry. I'm Swing, your new bosun. I am from New
Jersey but have lived in other places almost my whole life."

Alan couldn't believe it. Did he say Swing, just like Ham's com-
manding general?

Alan said, "I'm Alan."

Swing said, "Where's Cal?"

Neither Alan nor Bud knew where Cal was. Alan hadn't seen
him since the galley discussion with Rosie. Bud hadn't seen him since
he left the *Demson* with the captain in Cleveland.

The deckhands said almost at the same time, "We haven't seen
him."

Swing ordered us out of bed and to muster at the tool crib at
the aft end of the boat. He turned around and headed up the stairs.
Swing made it to the wheelhouse in less than a minute.

Swing declared, "Cal is missing. The deckhands don't know where he is."

Briggs said, "I'll call Brads. He is with Lil in his cabin."

Then Briggs used the house phone and called Brads's cabin. "Brads, this is Briggs. Cal is missing. He didn't go to bed last night."

Brads said, "What? That's impossible. He must be on board somewhere. Look for him."

Brads hung up. Brads looked at Lil, and she guessed what he was going to say.

Lil said softly, "Cal is missing, right?"

The captain said defeatedly, "Right."

The next hour was frantic. The entire crew, including Lil, turned the *Demson* inside out and looked in every spot Cal could be. They came up short, with no sign of Cal. The search began to take an ugly turn as the bosun's quarters were reviewed. Hard Rock had left behind a note reading, "I am gone but I won't forget what happened."

Lil was very upset, and the captain was worried.

An announcement came over the intercom, "Captain, to the bridge."

When Lil and the captain came into the bridge, everyone was silent. Lil began to openly weep. The captain's eyes welled up.

Lil said what everyone one thinking, "He went overboard."

Briggs said, "The phone is for you. It's the *Branford's* captain."

Brads said, "Hello."

The voice on the other end was speaking, but no one could hear what he was saying. Brads said, "Thanks. Can you put him on?"

The voice said something.

Brads said, "Lil, Cal is okay. He is on the *Branford* and wants to speak with you."

Lil was relieved as was the entire bridge crew.

Cal said, "Hi, Mom. I'm sorry for the worry."

Lil said, "That's okay. You are safe, right?"

"Physically yes, emotionally not so much," admitted Cal. "I want to go home."

Lil looked at Brads and asked, "Can Cal go home?"

Brads said, "Yes, and I will make arrangements for a bus ticket. He will beat you home."

Lil said tenderly, "Yes, get off at the Soo and take the bus home. We can talk when I get there."

She passed the phone back to Brads. He gave his thank-you and apologies to the bridge crew on the *Bradford*. Brads hung up.

Brads thanked everyone. Lil and the captain made their way off the bridge and down into their cabin.

Lil was livid with the captain, but you would never know it. They were, at least in public, cordial and kind. You could hear them laugh and see them smile as they made their way around the freighter. It was like they were are a pleasure cruise.

In private, the two were having serious conversations about Cal, the wedding, and the outfall from the past several weeks. The captain committed to be more involved with the wedding and to let Cal and Bud have the time of their lives. Lil was doubtful but agreed to see how things progressed.

CHAPTER 26

· · · · · · · ● · · · · · · · · ·

THE TRIP NORTH

*Alan slipped around the corner to his position
on the bulkhead. As he lifted his brush to paint,
a wave came over the rail and up the deck.*

Alan asked Bud, "Are you getting married to the captain's daughter?"

Bud reluctantly replied, "Yes, we weren't supposed to tell you our relationship with Brads."

Alan said matter-of-factly, "That's totally understandable. Hey, did you catch the new bosun's name, Swing?"

Bud said, "No, he said Steve."

Alan said, "I am sure he said Swing, but I will ask again."

Alan knew that this was the second time the bosun's name seemed different to him than what the others heard. *Is this another ghostly appearance?* "No," Alan said to himself, "General Swing is not dead."

Alan thought that maybe he was just being affected by Ham's telling of his war story. Alan promised to keep his imagination in check.

The crew finally ate breakfast and were ready to begin work as they were leaving the St. Clair River. It had been a tough couple of days, and it felt good to be out into the open water. The wind was up, and the crew was painting the bulkhead walls on the aft cabin.

Bud was painting the front wall of the aft cabin, and Alan was on the starboard side. The chief engineer waved Alan over. He asked if Alan wanted to come inside his cabin. Alan was a bit leery and declined, but the chief insisted.

As Alan walked in the darkness of the cabin, it blinded him. He couldn't see anything. As his eyes became adjusted, he could see several pairs of red eyes looking back at him. He was startled and fearful.

The chief laughed and said, "These are bats. They are not pets. That would be against company policy. I use them to keep the flying insects away."

Alan was not impressed and backed out of the cabin. "Thanks for the show, Chief," Alan exclaimed.

The chief said something, but Alan didn't hear it. "You are an ungrateful grandson of the Cap'n." The chief worked with Cap'n many times over the years.

Alan walked around the corner to join Bud.

"Bud, the chief has bats," Alan explained. "I don't ever want to go into that guy's room again!"

Lunch was great; they had fried chicken and vegetables. After lunch, the bosun told them to return to their painting. The boat had shifted its course as planned but that wind conditions were then different as well.

Alan slipped around the corner to his position on the bulkhead. As he lifted his brush to paint, a wave came over the rail and up the deck. It was of such volume and force it took Alan's paint can, brush, scrapper, and drop cloth over the side. Alan had water in his boots as the wave came over the top of his feet all the way up to his ankles. The wave pulled at Alan, and he came to the very edge of the deck before he could stop himself from going overboard by grabbing the wire rope which served as a rail.

Alan pulled himself up on his feet and went around the corner just as another wave hit the side of the freighter. Alan yelled, "Did you guys know I was going to attacked by the waves. It isn't funny!"

Bud and bosun simply looked at him bewildered.

"Why are you all wet?" asked the bosun.

Alan explained but to no avail. It was dry where they were, and the soaking Alan got seemed unrealistic.

"Okay, help us finish here and we will do the other side tomorrow," the bosun offered. It was a great change of tone for Alan.

That night, they made the Soo. They also picked up two deckhands, Jack and Ray. The names seemed quite familiar to Alan, but he kept it to himself. One deckhand replaced Cal, the other replaced Alan. Alan was going to work as a deck watch for a week as the second shift deck watch took a leave to see his ill mother.

Alan's new role didn't begin until the next afternoon. On that day, he had Lake Superior for himself. He looked out to the horizon. There was nothing but forty-degree water and the sky.

Then it seemed like a miracle happened. They headed toward the shore of the upper peninsula of Michigan. The entered the passage way for the Keweenaw Peninsula, the appendage sticking out of the land mass called the Upper Peninsula of Michigan. It can be a safe harbor for ships in a storm.

Captain Brads promised Lil that they would go through the passage the next time she was aboard. This was the right time as they made plans for their future with their family. The passage isn't long. It has high hills, with small lake in its middle, and the green forests are so close they seemed like it was right out of a picture book.

As they left the passage, Alan could imagine Isle Royal to the north of the boat. It is a national forest with no vehicles allowed on its shore. It was a great day for Alan.

He read a little and rested. It seemed like this was his best day since he began his summer, and he hadn't had much time off to simply watch the waves.

As the afternoon waned, he reported for duty. The first thing he had to do was make coffee. He never drank coffee, and he certainly never made it. The wheelsman explained the process to him, and he followed every word.

When completed, Alan was asked to take soundings. This task offered the deck watch an opportunity to walk down the deck and take a piece of chalked rebar about five feet long with painted markings on its side every six inches. The bar is attached to a rope through an iron eye at the end of the steel rod. Alan dropped the rod down a hole on deck into the ballast tanks. The idea was to determine the depth of the water to see if the levels were changing. The process was repeated six times per side of the boat. The depths were recorded and delivered to the wheelhouse.

"Alan, you idiot!" the wheelsman proclaimed. "No water in the pot! You're going to burn the pot up! We have no coffee!"

Alan apologized. He took the pot and redid the process and made sure there was water in it. When he returned, everyone had a cup of coffee they were sipping and simply chuckling to themselves. Alan deduced that this was what they did to the new guy.

The wheelsman said to the second mate, "It looks like we are taking on water in the ballast tanks. The water levels are creeping up. I have noticed the trend ever since we left Cleveland. I think that the rivets on the hull may have loosened while we were galloping."

The second mate said, "We will watch it and keep the jockey pumps on for safety."

"Aye, aye, mate," repeated the crew.

Alan's final task of the shift was to take the soundings again. It was dark, and the only light on deck were the standards near the rails every fifty feet or so. When the daylight assisted him, he could find the holes for the tanks easily. The task of chalking the rod and send it down to the ballast tanks was clear. The recording of the measurements was performed skillfully, and the entire task was finished with ease.

Now it was dark. The water had become a dark blue-black. The waves seemed so close. He could hear the wind howling. He knew if a wave came over the side like it did that day he was painting, he would be swept in. He would die in a few minutes after he hit the water, and no one would miss him for maybe thirty minutes. It was dark, and it would be impossible to find him anyway.

The first sounding took forever. Alan knew now why it was important to get it right. It had become apparent that the freighter is taking on water. He finished the first sounding, and he thought he saw something or someone in the water. No, it was his imagination again. He looked again. Was it a giant creature? He shook his head as he closed his eyes. The boat seemed to be rocking. He was losing his balance. He opened his eyes and gained composure.

He had eleven soundings to go. He struggled to go on deck between the lights into the darkness. Alan made it through the port side ballast holes; now he had to go over to the starboard side. The blue-black waters were simply terrifying. He completed all, but the last sounding and a voice from afar yelled to him. Alan looked into the blackness and couldn't see anyone. A hand grabbed him from behind, and he froze.

The next deck watch was coming on duty, and he wanted Alan to know that he was relieved. Alan finished the last sounding and took the data to the wheelsman. Alan went to the bunk room and noticed all the beds were filled. He went to the library and lay down trembling until morning.

CHAPTER 27

THE TURNAROUND

He was terrified but continued to walk
the blue-black waters at night.

The *Demson* arrived at the break wall of Duluth by mid-morning. The unloading was especially important to keep pace with the schedule because so much time was lost in Cleveland. The new deckhands were skilled but still needed guidance through their paces. The loading was finished in eight hours. Right on schedule. The clear skies helped a lot.

While the boat was in dock, Alan had a break for the first time. He went ashore after asking the first mate for twenty dollars to be deducted from his account at the end of the summer. With the money, he bought a large knife for Ham. That way, Alan thought, he could have Ham send the World War II samurai sword back to its rightful family.

The deck clearing was undertaken, and the hatch closings were completed. The whole process was completed as they made the break wall heading for Chicago.

Everyone always asked when they would arrive at the Soo or the next port after being underway for a while. Alan thought he would do something about the nagging issue of not knowing when the boat would arrive at the next stop. He met with the Swede and took down as much information as possible as to the distance and the time it took to go from one port to the next. Alan made a data log of the information, and with some calculations, he was ready to make a tool.

Alan then took a box and cut two circles out of its sides. The circles were concentric with one being twenty-four inches in diameter and the other being twenty-two inches in diameter. He connected the two at their centers with a fastener.

Alan wrote the names of all the ports the *Demson* would visit and the Soo around the edge of the large circle. On the smaller circle, he wrote the names of all the same ports and the Soo. About halfway up the small circle and above all the writing, he cut one small square. When he lined up the two ports coming from and going to, he wrote the distance and time to travel in days and hours in the square.

On the inner circle, he also had a clockface but not with hours, but days of the week around the face. In between the days were marks for three shifts of eight hours each. So when you knew your destination, you could find the duration for the trip from the information in the square.

Then using the clock hands also connected in the center of the circle, knowing what day and shift you left port, you could position the hands to determine the day and shift you would arrive in port.

The entire device was painted green with black letters. It was a hit. The questions were the same, but the answers were forthcoming and accurate.

Alan continue to work as a deck watch. He continued to make coffee. He was terrified but continued to walk the blue-black waters at night. The difference was he now was right on top of the water with a loaded vessel. It was almost hallucinating as he could see sea monsters with every step. Giant serpents were in the water along the boat's edge.

The galley was his best place to visit and be seen. Alan overheard the deckhands talking about the lottery. Alan wondered what the importance was but picked up in conversation that the lottery for the Army draft would be held that night for Alan's birth year. This was important.

When the *Demson* reached Chicago, the crew would get the results and determine the fate of a couple of the deckhands who were the same age, Alan being one of the two.

The trip down through the locks and the St. Marys River was foggy. When Alan's shift came up, he spent all his time on the bow, looking for interferences and other boats. There was no collision, but the stress and strain of searching in the fog for anything that might harm the boat was a tiresome activity. It was one that Alan was glad was behind them when they went under the Mackinaw Bridge.

The length of the trip to Chicago seemed long to Lil as she was anxious to get home. She had several last-minute plans to complete before the wedding. She also had a son who needed her, and she wanted to resolve the issues she had with him before the captain came home a week later for the wedding. The weather was cloudy, but there wasn't any rain.

The deckhands were hammering away at the windless room floor to paint it. While Alan tried to sleep, the hammering continued on the ceiling. The floor on the windlass room was the same steel deck as the ceiling of the deckhands' bunk room. The hammering was so difficult to sleep through; Alan got a headache, had ringing in his ears, and ended up in the library to sleep. The bosun entered the room.

"Alan, how is it going?" Swing asked.

"I'm fine, but I have a bit of a headache from the pounding and scrapping," Alan replied. "I do have to ask you a question. Are you called Swing or Steve?"

"Swing," the bosun replied. "I wanted you to recall that the commander has a tough task of deciding what action he would send his guys into and how they would survive during difficult situations."

Alan wasn't thrown off his thought. "I know the others know you as Steve, right?" Alan replied. "Why the difference?"

Swing said, "You will know why soon. I will leave you alone, but remember the commander has the responsibility to make tough decisions. By the way, I drink a little and I wanted you to know that fact about me. Don't judge me."

The crew had roast beef and biscuits for dinner that night. Bobby was singing a brand new blues song called "In the Summertime." "In the summertime when the weather is hot, you can stretch right up and touch the sky. When the weather's fine, you got women, you got women on your mind." Bobby was a good singer, and everyone smiled and tapped their toes or fingers.

They all went to bed while Alan was out on the deck surrounded by black water, taking soundings. Alan asked the wheelsman how the trends were going in the ballasts. The wheelsman said, "We are barely keeping up with the water intake using the jockey pumps, but we are pushing fifteen knots per hour in the open water." A knot per hour is 1.15 miles per hour. At higher speeds with wave action, more power was needed to move the loaded boat.

"Are we going to sink?" asked Alan.

"Not today," said the wheelsman. "Not today."

Alan knew what foreshadowing was from literature classes he had taken. He didn't like the reference the wheelsman was making.

CHAPTER 28

CHICAGO AND THE DRAFT

Alan splashed into the slip. He let go of the bosun's
chair and began a frantic swim back to the dock.

The south slip of the Chicago Steelworks was where Alan first arrived on board the *Demson*. It was the port where Lil and Bud would leave the freighter and head back to Cleveland by train. It was where the deck watch would return to relieve Alan. It was where the future of Alan's military fate would be known.

Lil was excited to leave this trip behind her. The captain and Lil had a great time, and he promised to be more present when he was with the family. He also promised to make time for and give space to Cal. He wanted to become a more complete parent to Cal and not just a disciplinarian. He wanted Cal to come first more often and would put Bud a bit on the side at times. Choices should be more to Cal's advantage. Lil was happier. The trip through the Keweenaw was a great start.

Lil packed her things and had breakfast with Brads. She said, "I will see you in a week. It will be fun having you home in the summer even if it is for just a little while. Sis will be happy to have us all at her wedding. Let me collect Bud and we will be off."

As they stepped out onto the aft deck, the *Demson* was coming into the slip. After a quarter of a mile, a deckhand would be dropped onto the dock by bosun chair. He would pull the tagline in until the steel line was in his hands. He would slip the steel line over the spar on the end of the dock and the boat would winch it in, pulling the bow of the boat into the dock. This would make the boat take a right angle using the dock as its fulcrum. Once the boat was beginning its turn, the steel line would be moved to a spar up the dock and pulled forward. This was tricky and the timing important.

Alan was the most seasoned deckhand with Bud leaving and Alan returning to his deckhand role. Alan would be the deckhand lowered to make the transfers. Swing was taking his time with the rigging. When he said ready, Alan climbed onto the chair, which was a flat board with the rope between his legs.

They crew lowered him down. As the boat continued to move forward, it was becoming apparent that Alan was not going to make a landing onto the dock but into the water. Alan splashed into the slip. He let go of the bosun's chair and began a frantic swim back to the dock. There was no ladder at the point he arrived at the dock, but he looked down the dock and saw one about fifty feet away. He swam to the ladder fully clothed and lost his yellow broad-brimmed hard hat along the way.

Alan climbed the ladder and ran back to the end of the dock. The tagline was thrown to him, and he caught it with maybe twenty feet of line to spare. As the boat moved forward, the line was quickly slipping through his hands. He grabbed it tight and began to pull. The weight of the steel line was much more than he had ever pulled before due to the distance the *Demson* had traversed.

Alan place his feet at the base of the spar and pulled with both arms. He was making progress, but it was clearly a struggle. The eye of the line was finally in his hand and then over the spar. The winch was started, and the boat began to turn the corner. It was a long sweep, and it took several minutes for the momentum to shift. Once the corner was made, Alan, still cold and wet from his dunk into the slip, lifted the cable and pulled it to the next spar. The boat straightened out, and the line was taut as the winch worked to tighten the line fully back to the boat. Alan ran down the dock to the point where the boat would berth, and the lines were pulled to the final spar. Alan had help by then with another deckhand lowered to the dock for the aft line.

Alan yelled up, "What the heck!"

The captain and Lil saw the whole maneuver. They both were quite complementary of Alan's actions and bravery.

The ladders were set, and Alan climbed aboard to change his clothes, but not his boots. But he remembered to change his socks, so his feet wouldn't "rot."

Lil and Bud climbed down the ladder and left through the large doors in the side of the mill. Bud had a special prize with him. He had taken the port side lifeboat's compass. He felt that it was never used, and no one would miss it. Later, the deck watch, Alan's relief, appeared through the same door. The deckhands tended the lines and took turns eating the whitefish on the menu for the day.

The day was uneventful compared to the events of the landing. The weather had become quite hot, raising the temperatures on deck to over hundred degrees. The coal in the bunkers were a concern with these temperatures with potential hot spots. The watchman and deck watch were hosing the coal with water when they saw a rise of smoke.

When the ore was unloaded, orders came to wash down the holds as well as the decks. The *Demson* was going to take on a load of coal. The coal was destined to go to a small reloading facility on an island near the top of the lower peninsula of Michigan near the mouth of the St. Marys River.

The wash down was hard and tedious. The ore that remained in the holds had to be washed to one side and then loaded onto the same clamshells that took the ore out of the holds. When that effort was finished, the last of the ore was shoveled into wheelbarrows. The work concluded with repeating this cleaning effort two more times.

Then the coal was loaded into the holds. This work was spotty because it wasn't a function performed every day. It took awhile, and the lines on the boat had to be moved several times to get a balanced load. When this was completed, the boat was moved up the slip, repeating the events of the previous morning, but without incident.

Finally, out into the open water, the boat was hatched and washed down. This was a very long day but one that had an unexpected ending.

After dinner, the deckhands went to their cabin. The had gotten a *Chicago Tribune* paper that had all the selective service lottery numbers by birth date. They opened the pages and found June 23, Jack's birth date. The lottery number was forty-four. This was a sure bet he would be drafted. November 13 was Alan's birth date. The lottery number was 272. Another sure bet, there would be no draft for Alan. Ham wouldn't have to worry that Alan would have to go to Southeast Asia. Alan bet that Ham already knew.

The crew celebrated Alan's fortune by creating a wooden plaque with the number 272 painted in black with three-inch-high numbers.

CHAPTER 29

UNLOADING COAL AND BASEBALL

Ray didn't like the self-umpiring idea
and bickered with every call.

The ride up Lake Michigan was hot, but it rained off and on. The new deckhands were not a cohesive group. Ray was a hothead. Everything was an affront to him, and he would let you know it. Jack was fine but simply didn't like to work. He would find a way to go get a tool right after he stopped to take a leak. Alan would out work both of the deckhands but was not happy with their demeanor and effort.

The coal load was being watched routinely by the deck watch and watchmen. Hot spots were a concern. They always had their water hoses at the ready to put out a smoker. The deckhands worked on the forward deck, painting the bulkheads white. The ballast soundings continued to show a rising trend, with water intrusion occurring at a faster rate.

The *Demson* made it to the coal facility in the afternoon of the following day. Ray and Alan tied up the boat, and Ray didn't like Alan's method of pulling the lines and let him know it. Ray came over to Alan after the lines were secured and said, "You are a show-off. A one-arm pull? Are you crazy! You're going to get hurt and put both of us at risk."

Alan said, "It's the most comfortable for me."

Ray pulled up to Alan's face and said, "Knock it off!"

They parted, but not settled.

The unloading was torturous. One clamshell lift at a time and the rate of emptying the boat was very slow. The captain was annoyed and let everyone know it. "I am on a tight schedule. I have a wedding to attend. Let's move it faster." The rate didn't change, but the captain saw everyone trying.

After nine hours, the boat was cleared to go. While underway, the coal was cleaned out of the hold by hand and lifted bucket by bucket out of the belly of the boat. The wash down occurred after and had to use the Jockey pumps to get the water out of the holds. This, in turn, strained the ballast-pumping effort. The next soundings were higher than ever.

After the decks were cleared and hatches secured, the crew went to a dinner of steaks and then to the holds to play baseball. The holds were open space fifty feet by fifty feet by one hundred twenty-five feet. The holds were clean, and regular balls and gloves were used. It was a bit like home run derby, but after a couple of hours, everyone had a great time, except for Ray.

Ray didn't like the self-umpiring idea and bickered with every call. Finally, Frankie and the Swede couldn't take it anymore. Frankie screamed, "I quit."

Ray came charging at Frankie, and the Swede stepped in between them. Ray hit the Swede. Then Alan stepped in and said, "Knock it off!"

Ray remembered the phase from earlier and really got angry.

Just then, Briggs came down the stairs and said, "How's it going? I love this about our boat, baseball as we travel."

Ray backed off and said it was just a game and left. That broke up the party, and everyone went to bed.

Alan remembered that baseball is a metaphor for life. The lesson he learned that day was not everyone likes to play by the same rules, not everyone wins, and not everyone is happy in the end.

• • • • • • • • • ● • • • • • • • • •

LAKE SUPERIOR CROSSING

*He let go of his tool and reached
back for the rail and missed.*

The day began with Swing getting the crew up. He was cheerful. He said, "With clean holds, we also have clean bulkheads under the hatches. We are going to paint them today. So get up and have breakfast."

The three deckhands made their way to the galley. Rosie was taking orders and Bobby was cooking. Again, he was singing, and Rosie joined in. They were singing the "Boxer" by Simon and Garfunkel. "I am just a poor boy, though my story's seldom told. I have squandered my resistance for a pocket full of mumbles, such are promises."

The mood was lifted, and the breakfast was satisfying. Swing said, "Let's go. The hatches need painting."

The Swede said, "We never paint the hatch bulkheads while we are underway. We never paint them when the holds are empty. Two guys fell earlier this year performing this task under these very conditions. They both died."

Swing was taken aback. He didn't change his mind, but he did say, "We are going to be careful."

The operation was to take a spud bar with a flat end and lift the hatches up and toward the center of the boat. The hatch bulkhead is then exposed to be scrapped and painted. The paint color is white and not to be spilled on the red deck. That means a drop cloth is necessary after the hatches are lifted out of the way.

Alan was working the spud bar with Ray, and the painting was primarily finished by Jack. After the painting was done, the hatch was lifted back in place with the spud bar going under the lip and lifting while pulling.

Three of the hatches were completed when the sky turned gray and it began to rain. Jack had finished his work, and Ray and Alan began to lift the hatch cover back in place. Alan's bar slipped, and he began to fall backward. The distance from the hatch to the steel wire rail was about two feet. Alan quickly hit the wire rope, and the upper stand was thigh high. He let go of his tool and reached back for the rail and missed. His body weight was now over the edge, and he was looking over his shoulder at the water fifty feet below. He knew as he was falling they it meant certain death when he went into the water.

Ray reached out quickly, and Alan thought he was just about to give him a shove based upon last night's baseball game and his anger. A hand quickly came up. Ray grabbed Alan's coat right in the middle of his chest. Ray clenched his fist. He pulled Alan in with one arm.

Alan could have died. Ray could have complained. Neither of these things occurred.

Alan said, "You saved me." Alan smiled as he continued, "I am so grateful for your one-arm pull. Maybe one-arm pulls are okay?"

Ray laughed and said, "Maybe."

The work was done, and the rain was steady. They dried and put their tools away. They all went to lunch. Alan was shaken and couldn't get the near-death experience out of his mind. He had so much to live for.

Swing apologized for the incident. He said, "Those in command make choices for others. They put them at risk. But it must be worth it if the risk is taken."

The afternoon was spent doing odd chores in preparation for the loading operation.

The soundings continued. The boat was definitely taking on water. The jockey pumps were barely keeping up, but the captain was on a schedule. He promised to be home for the wedding.

The weather had turned decidedly for the worse. The winds were gusting. The weather report showed a huge low coming in from the west. The rain was now more on and steady than off and drizzling.

"Alan?" Swing whispered.

"Yes?" replied Alan.

Swing then stated his intentions, "This is going to be a hard period we are coming into. I intend to stay in Duluth when we arrive. I don't believe the captain is making good decisions."

Alan asked, "Are you saying I should get off the *Demson*?"

"No," Swing declared. "You have to follow through with your destiny. It is your future and you have a right to live it."

Swing reminded Alan, "Just remember what I have said to you."

Alan thought that this advice sounded much like Hard Rock.

The rain got worse and the winds bellowed.

The *Demson* and her crew made the break wall at Duluth in good time and in pretty good shape. The loading operation began with the deckhands being dropped to the dock. They tied up the boat and climbed to the main deck to have dinner. It was a hearty soup with beef tips. Bobby outdid himself.

CHAPTER 31

THE FINAL LOADING

"There is a list, captain," stated Briggs, the first mate.

The loading machines were operated such that no one on the dock had to move the boat and tend lines. Alan and other deckhands were grateful. The loading operation continued for about ninety minutes, and then a loud bang came from the machine's engine. The loading machine couldn't move. The operators on the ground began to climb the rig and try to discover what went wrong. It took them over an hour to determine that the engine was blown and not repairable. A replacement engine would have to be brought by truck from the warehouse about ten miles away. A crew would have to be called out and the replacement would take approximately fifteen hours to perform, if the weather cooperated.

As the discussion continued, a large crack of thunder, simultaneously clapped as a lightning bolt, lit up the sky over the loader. The crew scrambled down and said we have to wait thirty minutes before we can go up again. If another lightning bolt was seen, the clock would start over. Thirty minutes passed and then another; finally, the all clear was given and men climbed the machine. It was lit with huge spotlights, and everything below had a glowing yellow tone.

After further inspection, it was determined that the loader was inoperable and couldn't move. The mechanics crew that will replace the engine refused to work in the downpour. Time was moving by at a clip that caused the captain to be very upset. The captain yelled, "C'mon! Is there nothing we can do? We can't afford to lose more time!"

The Duluth-based loading team decided that the boat could be shifted forward and aft to load the taconite ore in a pattern that would level the load in the holds. Taconite is an ore that has been rolled into tiny marbles. The deck and dock will be covered with marbles after a while, and the conditions of the night were not going to get any better.

The deckhands would have to work the entire loading operation with only breaks through the rotation of Alan, Jack, and Ray. The rain and the taconite would fall on them and hit their hard hats as they tended the lines hour after hour.

As the night came upon them, they walked the boat forward and aft. They were stiff with the cold and soaked to their skin. The temperature dipped into the forties, and it was taking its toll. The loading operation was supposed to take about eight hours. With the boat only half loaded, nine hours had already passed. The captain was frantic.

The captain ordered the loading to be completed by hold and not to shift the boat except to move to the next hold. The first hold to be completed was the aft hold, then the center and, finally, the forward hold.

"There is a list, Captain," stated Briggs, the first mate. "The boat is off-balance. She's listing five degrees to the port side. We're loaded, but we need to pause and move the load by hand. It will only take a few hours."

The captain replied, "No. We will use the ballast tanks to correct for it. The starboard side will be filled to compensate. Let's get going. We've lost over six hours which will be difficult to make up."

The holds had been open to the rain about fifteen hours. The jockey pumps now had the leaking ballast and the rainwater to eject from the holds; and the listing ballast water has to be maintained at a precise amount to avoid tipping.

The water past the break wall was being driven by the wind and was now howling at over fifty knots per hour. The waves were massive and the lake unforgiving.

The captain stated frankly, "I made a promise, and I will keep it."

The boat was released from the docks.

THE DESPERATE CLOSING

As the thirteenth hatch was being closed, a massive
wave came from an oblique angle to the boat.

The *Demson* was moving quickly out to the end of the break wall. The decks were dark with no lighting standards in place. There was taconite piled high on the decks and in between the hatches. The hatches were still in the loading position, and the crew was tried.

No, they were exhausted. They hadn't had much to eat, except as the rotations allowed, and the food was often cold or overdone, depending on what time the preparation process was in when the crew arrived at the galley.

The crew began to close the hatches. They had finished four, and the *Demson* made the end of the break wall. The boat immediately headed straight into the waves. The waves were massive, over thirty foot high. They were coming straight over the bow which was lower in the water due to the load she carried. The waves came down the gunnels onto the main deck and ran all the way down the decks, rolling off the port side.

Before one wave was off the boat, the next one hit. The crew was simply fighting wave after wave to close the hatches. The effort was time-consuming and dangerous. As the thirteenth hatch was being closed, a massive wave came from an oblique angle to the boat.

It hit a bit to the starboard side of the bow. The crew was swamped with the frigid water and held on. When it cleared, Frankie was gone. The blue-black water took him.

The Swede was in shock. He didn't expect any of this day's events, and to lose his best friend was simply overwhelming. He screamed to the wheelhouse, "You killed Frankie!" He shook his fist into the air. "I will hold you responsible!"

Alan didn't know that Frankie and the Swede were gay and that the loss of Frankie was more than just losing a close friend and coworker. What Hans, the Swede, had lost at that moment was more like losing a family member. Hans was inconsolable with anguish.

Alan stepped in and took Frankie's position on the winch with the Swede. The crew was now working shorthanded. The Swede tearfully yelled, "Why isn't anyone coming to help us?"

They managed to get another seven hatches closed, and another rogue wave came at them from the port side. Everyone held on to something attached to the deck. This time, no one was swept overboard.

Alan yelled, "Why are the waves so erratic?"

The Swede, now with some composure, yelled back, "We are in a cyclone! These are rare, maybe back to—"

Alan yelled, "1913!"

The crew was desperate. When out of the forward cabins came all the watchmen to help. The mates were also in tow.

The *Demson* was filling with water. The hatches were open, and the water was simply pouring in. The boat and its crew were in peril. The crew was now on an impossible mission to save their lives!

In a short period of time, the final hatches were closed, but the danger was not over. There were still no light standards in place and there was no sounding capability in the storm. There was no way to tell how high the water in the ballasts were. It didn't matter because the blue-black water of the lake was now surrounding the boat and lapping at its edges.

Alan and the crew were drenched and frozen. As they looked out from the forward deck to the aft, the boat appeared to be floating at the deck level. There was a limited distance from the deck to the waterline. The waves kept pounding on the bow, and the progress of the boat was slowed to nonexistent.

The boat was closed up, but recklessly vulnerable. Peril appeared on all sides. There was no view of any shoreline or any other vessel. The *Demson* was on its own.

Alan thought of his family. He thought of how Ham must have felt when his buddies were dying around him. Alan thought of Cap'n and the storm of 1913.

CHAPTER 33

• • • • • • • • • ● • • • • • • • • •

THE SINKING

He certainly would not go with Captain
Brads to an assured death.

The *Demson* was in trouble. Brads made difficult decisions based upon his promise to his wife, Lil, and his kids. Brads had risked everything for a timely arrival to the wedding of Sis and Bud. The boat and its crew are his responsibility. The perilous situation is his fault.

Brads shouted to the mates and wheelsman, "We are abandoning the *Demson*."

The first mate Briggs said, "Wait a minute. Is there no other way to make this right?"

The other mates chipped in:

"The jockey pumps are overwhelmed. The taconite load has shifted and it's only a matter of time that a wave will hit us and tip us more and shifting the load again. A final wave blast and that final tip will capsize us. We remember seeing pictures of one of the boats in the 1913 blow flipped entirely over."

"If the load tipping won't get us, the rivets on the side sheets will give way as they were loosened from the galloping vibration just north of Toledo after bottoming out at the edge of the Detroit River channel. This is the main reason for the ballast leakage."

"Then we overfilled the ballast tanks ourselves to counterbalance the listing and make the pumping challenge much harder."

"We have wave water in the holds due to the slow hatch closing and making the break wall too quickly. We are sinking."

Briggs said reluctantly, "We are done. Let's go."

Just as these words left his lips, a steel-buckling sound could be heard. The starboard side of the boat had buckled, and the port side had opened up.

The chief engineer called the wheelhouse and asked for the captain. "Captain, the bats have left my stateroom and flew off into the night. Goodbye!" he yelled over the roar of the wind and waves.

The captain came over the intercom, "Abandon ship! Abandon ship!"

Just then, Brads received a call from Alan's parents. Cap'n had died. Brads promised to tell Alan. In the crisis, he knew he couldn't keep that promise nor the one to Lil.

Brads called Lil and tearfully said, "I'm not going to make it to the wedding."

Lil said, "You are going to be late again. You promised me! I am so angry and disappointed in you."

Brads said, "I love you." He hung up.

Brads called, "Mayday, Mayday, Mayday." There was a response, but it was hard to hear. The voice on the other end wanted positioning and protocol information, but Brads just responded with, "This is Captain Brads of the *Demson*, and we are lost."

At the Coast Guard Station in Duluth, the limited information and lack of positioning placed a lifeboat rescue at risk and the chances of finding the small craft remote.

The Coast Guard radioman said, "Has the entire crew been lost, or did some make it away in a small craft?" There was no answer after numerous tries. "What is your location?" demanded the seaman.

The Coast Guard crew took the approach that some of the *Demson* crew made it onto a lifeboat. They needed to be found and rescued. The Coast Guard craft was launched into the heavy waves of Lake Superior. They too became endangered while executing their mission.

Back on the *Demson*, the forward crew members began to panic, but the aft crew members began to make the lifeboats ready to launch. As the aft crew loosened the starboard lifeboat, it broke free and was lost in the dark waters.

Alan was reliving the storied nightmare of 1913 his grandfather told him about.

Several crew members from the forward cabins of the boat worked their way on deck toward the aft end of the freighter. They were picked off the deck quickly and permanently in their attempt to escape the sinking boat by the massive and persistent waves.

Next came an effort for the remaining forward crew members to make their way along the inside passages next to the hull. The passages have no light, and between the hulls, there are steel hatches to pass through. They made their way to about halfway along the six-hundred-foot boat and found the hull bent to such a degree that they could not pass. The Swede Hans, Jack, Ray, Briggs, and the others could not turn around quick enough before the midship came apart and they were swallowed by the frigid blue-black waters.

Alan began to follow the crew down the starboard side that had been buckled. The inside passageway entry was at the same level as the deckhands' and bosun mate's rooms.

The young man grabbed a flashlight and the knife he bought for Ham from his dresser drawer and put it through his belt.

Alan heard a voice in the din of the storm. It was Captain Brads. "Come with me to the bridge," he screamed. "You'll never make it to the life raft. You can come with me and watch our final activities as it unfolds."

He heard another voice call out to him. He could have sworn it was Hard Rock, his first bosun mate. Then he recognized the man in the shadows as Swing. Alan was whirling with confusion.

Alan yelled, "I thought you were staying in Duluth? Okay, you're here, but why didn't you go down the starboard inner passageway?"

The voice said, "Let me remind you of a couple of things. I am your bosun. You do what I say, period! Ignore the captain. He is on his way down with the ship. I warned you to stay away from him to be safe."

Swing said, "I always said that if you have command, you make the tough decisions. You are all that you have right now, so make the tough decision."

"Okay, but what are my options?" Alan said as he drew closer to the bosun. Then he saw the bosun had lost a leg. Alan screamed, "How did that happen?"

The bosun said, "Never mind. You have but one decision. Go down the port side!"

"I won't leave you," Alan said as he heard the bells chime four times.

"Yes, you will," replied the bosun. The bosun struggled to move into his cabin. When he finally made it to the bed, Alan looked him in the eyes. In this new light, the man appeared to be his grandfather. "Cap'n, how could this be?" Alan implored.

However, this push toward the starboard side was a trend he was very aware of based upon his grandfather's experience. The boat was sinking, and he almost made a choice that his grandfather so wisely avoided. The trend of the activity around Alan indicated that he not blindly follow the crew to the starboard side of the freighter. He certainly would not go with Captain Brads to an assured death.

Alan was now creating his own future that was both understandable and predictable.

Alan jerked up from his position and ran past the captain and the bosun into the inside passage on the port side. Alan was strong and worked himself down the passageway with a flashlight in his hand. When he made it to the midship, he found a gaping breach about ten feet wide. Water was moving in as each successive wave hit. The steel bracing was a tangled mess over the gap. Alan began to cross the breach and was hit with another icy wave. Alan lost his flashlight but held on tight to the steel as the water rushed back out. He then proceeded in the dark. There was another gap with no steel bracing. Just as Alan reached across the gap, another icy wave hit. Alan breathed heavily as the wave felt like a sledgehammer on his side. He didn't let go. Alan leaped as the wave receded and gabbed the steel on the other side. Alan had made it past the opening.

Alan made his way alone and in the dark, through the hull to the opening at the aft end of the freighter. Water was rushing down the passageway from the stairs above. Alan fought his way up and out to the opening on the deck. Through the door, he saw the last of the aft crew dropping the port side lifeboat to the lake waters below.

He rushed to the pendant and rigging. As Alan peered from *Demson's* edge, the small boat was being battered by the waves against the hull of the freighter. Alan yelled and waved.

Bobby looked up slightly and saw him. Bobby shouted, "Jump, Alan! Jump now!"

Alan desperately looked toward the wheelhouse and saw the captain. He was dressed in the white shirt Rosie repaired, and the singular light behind him gave an eerie ghostlike impression similar to what Alan remembered about Charlie's room at the county hospital. There was another gaunt figure of a young man next to him also dressed in white. The figure had a transparency to his appearance, and Brads didn't seem to notice him.

Alan and the two men purposefully waved to each other. Then Alan jumped a few feet into the icy forty-degree water next to the boat.

Alan was immediately stiffened with cold. Rickie pulled Alan into the lifeboat and gave him a life vest.

As the survivors pulled on the oars toward what they thought was shore, Alan could see the *Demson* had come apart and sink so silently.

Alan knew no one could survive the frigid water. The captain and the bosun was gone. Alan shivered from the cold and the thought of their deaths. Any of the individual crew members was lost unless they made it in the lifeboat with Alan and the remaining aft crew.

No one else did. They would go to the bottom of the lake and not return to the surface. Lake Superior does not give up its dead. The very cold water slows down the bacterial breakdown of a corpse, eliminating the creation of gas, which would allow a body to float eventually.

Alan was in the right place at the right time because he was prepared. He listened, and he had the knowledge Cap'n had given him on his visit to the hospital. He still needed guidance from the mysterious bosun mates, and then that information came at a time when he needed it most. Not too soon and certainly not too late.

• • • • • • • • • ● • • • • • • • • •

CHAPTER 34

THE ENDING

Alan shouted, "Let's head in that direction."

The storm was still battering the lifeboat as they pulled on the oars. It was frightfully cold, and they were all soaked with forty-degree lake water. Alan thought about his feet and his wet socks and quite glad he could feel both of them. The dark night offered no light with the storm and its cloud cover.

"Let's get the compass out to see which way we need to go," offered Alan.

Bobby looked through the supplies and said, "There are flares and a map, but no compass."

Alan knew that without the compass there was no way they would know which was to go. The sky was as blue-black as the waters they were being tossed in. Alan remembered that Swing said, "With the responsibility of command comes tough decision-making."

Alan shouted, "Let's head in that direction. It is the opposite of heading into the waves like we did when we left Duluth. Besides, it will be easier rowing." Everyone laughed timidly and agreed.

The crew rowed for hours. The rowing made sure that they stayed aligned with the waves. The rowing used energy but also kept their inner body heat higher. They also controlled the lifeboat some-what such that no wave could capsize the small craft. The only breaks they afforded themselves were for a quick drink of water and grabbing a bite from the pouch the cook's crew brought from the galley. They were heroes.

The weather broke as morning appeared. The rain subsided, and the torrent of wind yielded. The small boat was heading west based upon the sun rising in the east.

Eight hours after the *Demson*'s sinking, they could see a white Coast Guard boat coming into view at the horizon and bouncing over the large waves.

The Coast Guard vessel had been out searching for the same eight hours. They had the advantage of knowing about where the *Demson* should be, but without any light on the blue-black waters, there was no quick way to see a tiny boat, let alone anything else. The crew of the Coast Guard was tired, wet, and cold.

Bobby shot a flare into the sky.

Rosie shouted, "Did they see it? Did they see us?"

The Coast Guard vessel didn't change course. The flare hung in the air but then dipped into the lake.

Alan yelled, "Bobby, shoot off another one!"

Bobby yelled back, "We have only one more."

Rosie shouted, "Then make it a good shot!"

The flare was shot into the air. It was a shot of fire. It left a trail of smoke. At the flare's highest point, its apex, the cutter steered toward them, and the *Demson* survivors knew they were saved.

Alan shouted, "We are saved!"

Everyone breathed a loud and heavy sigh of relief.

As the *Demson* crew made it onto the cutter, they all credited Alan for their safe passage from the *Demson* to their current position. They were disgusted that someone had taken the lifeboat compass and swore it was one of the forward crew members who didn't have a clue what disaster might befall them.

The survivors were nine in number. They included Bobby, Rosie, and Rickie. Tommie didn't make it as he had stayed behind to help others, if needed. It was a selfless act although futile. The captain, the chief, and all the mates were lost. One of the wipers survived as did all three of the licensed engineers and one oiler. The final survivor and only forward crew member was Alan.

The ride back to shore and Coast Guard Station was solemn. The cutter crew gave them coffee, which Alan didn't drink, and blankets to wrap around themselves. Rosie and Bobby shared a blanket as they prayed to God for their safekeeping. The waves were still rolling, but with much less intensity. The slow ride took about three hours. Alan didn't think that they had gone that far from the break wall at Duluth, but they were fighting the hull closing for a quite a while before the disaster set in.

The cutter crew was very curious as to what happened. One of the engineers began to tell his version of the story, but Bobby told everyone that no one was talking until they spoke with the Steel Company's representative. Bobby was a company man through thick and thin and to the end.

When Alan made it back to shore and had an opportunity, he called his mother and father. "Hi, Dad, Mom," he said softly and carefully. "We lost the *Demson* last night. I'm okay, but I am coming home. I'm in Duluth, and I should be home by bus tomorrow."

Elm said, "We thought you were calling because Cap'n died overnight. We radioed the *Demson* and talked to Captain Brads. He said he would let you know, but he said he was quite busy and had to go." Elm began to weep.

Ham grabbed the phone receiver and blurted in, "Cap'n died in his sleep."

Alan said in a matter-of-fact manner, "It was about four this morning."

Elm, listening close to the receiver in Ham's hand, took back the phone and gathered herself while taking a deep breath. Upon exhaling, she said, "That's right. How did you know?"

Alan said, "He visited me when the bells of the ship's clock sounded four times. He helped me through the inner passageway to the lifeboat, just as he did when his boat was sinking so many years ago. I am alive because of Cap'n."

Elm said, "I am not sure how that can be, but I am so grateful that you are alive. See you soon." She again had tears in her eyes from both for her father's death and also for her son that she help place in harm's way.

Alan said, "I will be home for the funeral. Can you put Dad on?"

Elm handed the phone back to Ham. Ham said, "Are you okay?"

"Yes," said Alan. "I have so much to tell you, but I have been with Hard Rock, Swing, and Cap'n." They all helped me through the ordeal. Hey, I got you a massive knife, so you can send back the samurai sword to its rightful family."

Ham said, "Slow down. We can talk all about it when you get home."

Then he paused and added, "Don't forget to get paid."

They both laughed.

Alan said slowly and loudly so both of his parents could hear, "Bye, Mom, Dad. I love you both."

THE AFTERMATH

*Alan was heartbroken over the loss of most
of the crew and all of the officers.*

"That call was difficult from a logistics perspective beyond the content of the call," Alan said to himself as he hung up the receiver.

A New Jersey man named Shaw claimed to invent the speakerphone in 1948. It would have been so much easier to have had the difficult conversation with all three parties on the phone at one time.

Alan said, "I understand being behind the technology curve, but wouldn't it be an important investment in my future successes if I could just be current?" This would be a lifelong theme going into his future.

Alan thought about the technology dilemma between having the newest technology and not having the money to buy it. He vowed to get a calculator before he finished engineering school.

Alan was heartbroken over the loss of most of the crew and all the officers. He knew that over time he would be able to apply the leadership lessons he learned from each of the men and Rosie throughout the summer.

Just like baseball, there were a limited number of survivors. The individual baseball teams had winners and losers. The sinking and escaping the *Demson* had its heroes and its goats. Some of the individual sailors were successful on one day and, on the next day, lost in the blue-black water. Those sailors that lived on carried the dismay and glory of the events. But of course, these individual men and woman made the story worth telling.

Alan took away several lessons from the ordeal.

He thought of the crew trying to get the lifeboats into the water. He remembered just how difficult and almost impossible it was to launch the boats. There were two lifeboats, but they lost one of the boats in the same way as over sixty years earlier. What if more forward crew members made it to the aft section of the freighter? Would there have even been room for all of them in the one remaining lifeboat? Why wasn't more done to prepare the crew for this necessary skill although unlikely to be used?

Alan said out loud, "It will be my responsibility to prepare myself and any team I lead for the challenges at hand."

If it were not for the crew, some of them now dear friends, and his family, he would not be alive. Alan needed Cap'n and his story when he survived the 1913 blizzard. He needed Swing and Hard Rock who meant so much to his father. He knew what not to do when thinking of Brad's leadership style. He was so thankful for the very least and best of the crew, who helped him into the lifeboat. Alan absolutely believed that you must depend upon your team, friends, and family because they will not let you down.

Alan realized that whatever he did from that point forward would affect his family. The long and strong connection with the culture and experiences of your past is a fundamental input to the way you will lead your life in the future. How you view things and your vision will assist you in problem-solving. They are also essential ingredients to the vitality of your life.

What Alan was most concerned about was the fact he actually talked to and saw men he knew were dead. This mystery was not lost on him, but he was so very glad that the intersection with these men occurred and to help shape his destiny.

Now in the light of day, Alan looked out at the bright blue waters and white-capped waves of massive Lake Superior and simply said, "Thank you."

Alan started to think about his plans when he returned home. He knew that ideas are not a plan, but they do help provide direction. He definitely wanted to be an engineer and maybe focus on improvement for workers and their working environment. If this was to be at least part of his life's purpose, then he would use it as a guide.

He rededicated himself to lay out specifics in this endeavor to more assuredly meet his goals. Having had the *Demson* experience, he knew he didn't want to be a sailor, but he could see that with the challenging and terrifying activity he just experienced, he could recheck his purpose for being a value-driven human being.

All the kindness the Swede provided Alan as a mentor will have a huge impact on his thinking and will act as an enduring guide over Alan's lifetime.

Alan welled up while smiling.

CHAPTER 36

NOT SO FAST

*The Coast Guard crew member said, "Slow
down. I'm Lieutenant Stevens."*

Alan stepped out of the Coast Guard office after making the
call to his parents. He looked around for a familiar face and
saw Bobby across the room. He had tears in his eyes. As Alan
approached, Bobby turned away sobbing.

Alan quietly asked, "What's wrong?"

Bobby said softly, "We are all under investigation. People have
died. We have to tell what happened and why we made it into the
lifeboat when so many others didn't."

Alan straightened up and boldly stated, "We can do that. We
did nothing wrong."

Bobby said, "I know, but Rosie was taken away by the police to
question her alone, and I don't know where she is."

Alan said, "Okay. Let's start by finding the people in charge. We
also need to find the six others from our crew."

The US Coast Guard and the National Transportation Safety
Board investigators were not completely on scene as they were still
being summoned to the Duluth Station.

Alan found one of the Coast Guard crew members who picked
up Alan and the other survivors of the wreck. Alan asked, "Who is in
charge? I would like to know if I can leave, and what is the process

for checking us out? By the way, where are my crew mates, and where have you taken Rosie?"

The Coast Guard crew member said, "Slow down. I'm Lieutenant Stevens. My captain, Brown, is currently in charge, and he is in his office right over there. He is arranging for hotels rooms and fresh clothes for each of you. Rosie was taken away first to Willard Munger Inn because she indicated she didn't feel well."

Alan interrupted, pointing to Bobby, "Bobby is her husband! Didn't you think to include him in your plans? Take him to her please. He has been through enough!"

Stevens immediately went to his captain. Bobby was whisked away to the same hotel as Rosie.

Stevens returned to Alan and said, "All the others are being detained for now, and that includes you. We want to talk to each of you independently to take your statement. People have died, and a great boat of the lakes has gone down. We want to know what happened. We owe an explanation to all parties concerned."

Alan's ears perked up. Where were the company personnel? It was their boat.

Alan asked, "Where are the Steel Company safety personnel and representatives?"

Stevens said, "They will be here shortly, and we don't intend to start any interviews until they are here."

Alan said, "I need to call my family again. My grandfather has died, and I was attempting to go to his funeral. I told them I was taking a bus home and would be there by tomorrow. I guess those plans are way off and wrong."

Stevens said, "Just wait until the Steel Company personnel and the government investigators arrive before you make that call. Let's make sure the plans are set before you make another false start."

Alan said, "Fine. Can I talk to my crewmates?"

Stevens said, "No. We prefer that everyone stays separated such that stories are not influenced by any of the others. It is not that we don't trust you, but our experience is that everyone remembers things a bit differently. Their experiences are different, and we want the recollection of each crew member to be pure and without influence by anyone else."

Alan said "Okay, I understand."

Alan felt the stress of the investigation rising within him already. He knew they did nothing wrong, but it felt like something was out of control.

Alan sat down and asked for something to eat and drink. A Coast Guard galley member brought him a hot plate of spaghetti and a glass of milk. It was good and satisfied his hunger. He was still a bit wet, and they offered him dry pants, socks, and shirt. He was taken to change in the locker room.

Alan was on one side of the lockers and overheard two Coast Guard crewmen come in. They were in heated conversation.

One of the men talking in a loud whisper said, "The deckhand is the only crew member from the forward portion of the boat to make it to the lifeboat. How did that happen? No one else made it to the aft. No one!"

Alan was now concerned. The focus was on him.

Alan left the locker room after the two men vacated. He went back to his chair. Suddenly, the room became quite active as the investigators and Steel Company representatives arrived.

The arriving personnel all went into a conference room and shut the door. Alan could see them talking, getting up to make a point, and sitting down again. After a period of time, the conference room door opened. The investigators looked around, and their eyes landed on Alan.

"Come in here," said an older man in a gray suit. "You are Alan, right?"

Alan indicated yes with a nod. Then he asked, "Who are you?"

The man simply said, "Come in."

CHAPTER 37

· · · · · · · · ● ● ● ● ● ● ● · · ·

THE INTERVIEW

Alan was very alert. He said with
confidence, "Yes, that's right."

A lan looked around the room. There were three men in suits in the room. The man in the gray suit seemed to be taking direction from the other two as he sat down at an end of the table. Alan was seated across from the other two men. The noticeably shorter and younger man spoke first, "Alan, I am Bob Carmichael. I am from the Steel Company and I am your representative in the interview. This is Rick Hamil"—he gestured to his right—"and down on the end is Mike Current, also from the Steel Company. He is a safety inspector. Rick works for the National Transportation Safety Board. Oh, here comes Captain Brown of the Coast Guard."

The door opened and in came a uniformed man in his forties. He reached out his hand to Alan. They men shook hands. "Alan," Captain Brown started, "please relax. Do you want anything to drink?"

Alan shook his head no.

"Okay, then let's get started," said Rick. "We have spoken to almost all your shipmates, except the chief cook and the assistant cook, who are resting at a nearby hotel. They didn't feel well, so we will talk to them in a little while.

"What we are trying to figure out is, why did the *Demson* go down? With all the survivors being from the aft end of the boat, except you, we want to learn what you saw. Also, why did you make it to lifeboat when no one else who worked on the boats for years was able to do what you did?"

"As we spoke to the other crew members, they indicated that they had some warning from the captain to abandon ship. They were trying to launch the starboard lifeboat but lost it as it bounced around in the waves next to the hull of the *Demson*. They said that they immediately went to the port side and launched it.

"They recalled that just as they were finishing loading the small craft, you appeared out of a stairway door and at the edge of the boat. They said you jumped into the water without fear and without a life vest. You were completely submerged, and you were stiff when they pulled you into the lifeboat. Does all that sound right?" Hamil concluded.

Alan was very alert. He said with confidence, "Yes, that's right."

"What lead up to the order to abandon ship?" Captain Brown asked politely.

Rick shook his head and leaned toward Brown and said, gritting his teeth, "I am leading this interview. Alan, don't answer that question."

Hamil asked with some tension in his voice, "Where were you when the order came to abandon ship?"

Alan, getting a bit nervous, gathered himself and said calmly, "I was just outside the deckhand's cabin with some of the other crew members."

"Were you aware of the peril you and the others found themselves?" Rick asked a bit less agitated.

"Yes," Alan pronounced. "We had been working through the twenty-hour period of the loading of the *Demson* in a torrential rain. The loading started about five in the morning, and by eleven that morning, the equipment had failed. Then we began loading the *Demson* by pulling the boat forward and aft by the winches. It was slow, so we began to load each hull fully until complete. This method was noted by the first mate to be a less careful way to balance the hulls from side to side and between hulls. We finished loading about one in the morning the next day.

"We left the docks and the break wall before we completed closing the hatches, which would be a normal practice. But with the storm, we were taking on water to the extent the main deck was almost level with the waterline. Adding the thirty-foot waves exploding over the bow to the mix, we knew we were at the very edge of safety."

Rick said, "You mean sinking?"

Alan explained, "We didn't know that at the time. We were desperately working to close the hulls up water tight."

Rick asked, "Did you see the captain?"

"Yes, briefly. He knew the boat was sinking and asked me to go to the wheelhouse with him," Allen said curtly.

Alan was shaken, and he began to ramble and tell his story a bit out of order. It was a bit hard to follow. "I noticed that he was agitated but didn't understand why. The last time I saw the captain was in the wheelhouse, looking out as I jumped into the water near the port side lifeboat. Earlier, after I and the other deckhands had been out in the weather for hours, the captain finally turned on the spotlights for everyone to see. Then out came additional help. I wondered at the time why it took so long for anyone to understand why it was taking so long. What I didn't understand was how unusual of a step it was in sending out other senior crew members to help close up the hatches."

Alan said, "I think the hulls were full of water. There was an accident with one of the propellers earlier in the month and the loosened rivets in the sheet steel of one hull allowed leaking into the ballast tanks. Additionally, with the rain and the waves, I think the hulls were saturated and full. I think the pumps to drain the hulls were overwhelmed. This was the essence of the sinking of the *Demson*."

Alan went on, "I think the taconite load had shifted. We were not very precise in the loading due to the manual operation using winches. The *Demson* was listing a bit and caused the boat to be hammered by the waves with no real maneuvering ability. It was a bit lucky we didn't simply go over on our side."

Alan added, "We had wave water in the holds due to slow hatch closing and making the break wall too quickly. I did hear steel buckling. I saw the starboard side of the boat cave in and the port side open up. Then the *Demson* sunk."

Bob Carmichael gasped. The company didn't want the accident to be laid at the poor decision-making of its captain. Their insurance claim to recoup cost associated with the lost vessel and her ore would be disallowed, but worst yet, the Steel Company would be liable for the lives lost.

Bob interrupted insistently, "Alan, are you saying the decisions being made by the captain were knowingly dangerous?"

Alan thought and said, "I don't know an answer to your question."

Bob repeated, "C'mon, you don't know or don't want to say?"

Alan thought again and repeated, "I don't know."

Rick said, "Let's stop here for a few minutes."

Alan asked, "I need to call my family. When can I tell them I will be on my way home?"

Captain Brown said, "You can use my phone, but it will probably be a few days until were done."

CHAPTER 38

CALLING HOME

*Alan said, "I get it. I am going to miss
my grandfather's funeral."*

Ham picked up the phone and said, "Hello."

Alan said, "Hi, Dad."

Ham inquired, "Are you on your way? What bus are you on? When and where should we pick you up?"

Alan held back a tear. "Dad, I am still in Duluth. There is an investigation. They are moving at their own pace, and I don't know when I will be home."

Ham yelled with a muffled receiver to Elm, "Alan is in the middle of an investigation on the *Demson* sinking. He will not be home for a few days at minimum."

"Alan," Ham went on, "look, don't worry about making the funeral for Cap'n. It wasn't something that was meant to be. It was important that you spent time with him before you left. You weren't supposed to be here anyway. You will be fine. Your mom understands. Things are a bit hectic for us right now."

Alan sobbing blurted, "I wish I was there. I miss you all!"

Ham encouragingly said, "I know, Mom knows. Alan, do you need any help? Do you need money or legal advice? When Rap had his near-miss accident, the company was a great help. You should confide in their representative. Hey, be honest."

Alan said, "Okay. I don't think I need anything. If I do, I will call again. Bye."

Ham said, "We love you. Bye."

Alan hung up and took a deep breath. Be honest. That is what he would always plan to do. He didn't have anything to hide.

He was rejuvenated and eager to get on with investigation.

Alan turned around to go toward the office door, and there stood Bob. Alan was taken aback.

Bob saw the shock on Alan's face.

Bob said, "I just walked in. I saw you hang up and wanted to catch you alone. I didn't hear anything about your conversation."

Alan quietly said, "Oh. I didn't hear you enter." Picking up the tone, Alan continued, "I am a bit off my game with the ordeal of the sinking and now the questions. Tell me, what is it that everyone wants?"

Bob said, "We simply want the truth. We want you to be forthcoming."

Alan chirped, "I have been."

Bob replied, "You took a long time to answer—I don't know—to the question of knowingly dangerous decision-making. You think something is off. We can tell in your demeanor. We know there may be a lot at stake here. For the insurance company, in dollars and cents. For the Steel Company, in reputation and liability. For the families, in answers to their questions. For the Coast Guard, in what was their role in placing anyone in peril. For you, why?"

Alan said, "I get it. I am going to miss my grandfather's funeral."

Bob shrugged. "I know it is tough. That's what sailors do, miss important events. I will arrange for flowers from you for the funeral. I will contact your grandmother and get the details. I owe her a call anyway. What do you want on the card?"

Alan said, "The 1913 blow and my survival. Thanks, Alan."

CHAPTER 39

THE SECOND TRY

Alan said, "The captain is in charge."

The five men reassembled in the conference room. They were Hamil, Brown, Carmichael, Current, and of course, Alan.

They all took the same seats as before. The investigators had met while Alan phoned home and planned their questions. Rick took the lead, but everyone this time was in alignment.

The formality was removed with the exiting of their jackets and ties, except for the captain. He remained in uniform because he was on duty and it was a perceived regulation. Captain Brown apologized for the formality of his dress.

This was going to be different.

Rick asked, "From an insurance perspective, who is at fault for the sinking of the *Demson*?"

Alan said, "I would think that they signed off on the repair to the propeller repair, and who knows what inspections they did on the hull after the accident? I would say that if that inspection was completely and properly finished, the loose rivets and the water leakage into the ballast tanks would have been known."

Rick asked, "If that were true, would the captain be the ultimate decision maker as to the seaworthiness of the *Demson*?"

Alan quickly replied, "Only if he had all the information. Were the records shared with him? Did he know of the hull weakness? He did have ballast soundings that showed the influx of water, but the jockey pumps were keeping up to a degree."

Rick said, "He knew of the influx?"

Alan replied, "Yes. I took a number of the soundings myself."

Rick went on, "The captain knew of the water leakage."

Alan retorted, "Yes, but if properly presented, so did the insurance company."

Rick said, "But they didn't know of the heavy seas and the hull closing."

Alan said, "In my opinion, it didn't matter. The hull buckled. I think the insurance company has some culpability."

"What about the Steel Company? What is their responsibility?" Hamil continued.

Alan said, "The captain is in charge. He hires the crew or agrees with their assignment to his vessel. The Steel Company drives the schedule and commits to production based upon it. The captain must deliver or feel the wrath of the officers of the company. The company has to take responsibility for the actions of the crew and its officers. Was there any ulterior motive in setting the schedule or pushing the crew? I don't know."

"What about the Steel Company?" asked again by Hamil.

Alan insisted, "The company has responsibility for the safety of the crew and its cargo."

Current, the safety man for the Steel Company, asked, "What do you think was unsafe about this incident?"

Alan replied, "We didn't wear life vests during the closing operation. It probably didn't matter because when crew members went over the side, they were lost. We could make no attempt to rescue them as the lifeboat was not launched at that time and the *Demson* was sinking. We could have used more help and lights sooner in the hatch closing, but that was an officer decision."

Current said, "There is probably more to add, but that's a good answer."

Hamil picked up where he left off, "Where did the Coast Guard fail?"

Alan said thoughtfully, "They were great. They didn't give up, and when the picked us up, they cared for us and didn't admonish us."

Brown said, "Thanks."

Hamil asked, "What should we tell the families?"

Alan said, "Before we continue, I would like to use the restroom."

THE INTERVIEW CONTINUES

Alan said, "It makes perfect sense."

Alan returned from his requested break and sat down.

Rick said, "I am going to ask a different question. What do you think was motivating Captain Brads's decision-making?"

Alan was taken aback. Why this question? What would be the reason for this particular question?

Alan asked, "Why?"

Rick said, "Look, I am trying to find out why Brads left the safety of the Duluth break wall."

Alan said quickly, "I don't know. But I am willing to think it through with all of you. First of all, he loved his family but had a tough time with the relationship he had with his son, Cal. Cal worked with us on the *Demson*, as did Bud, their future son-in-law and brother-in-law."

Bob said, "I knew of Cal's relationship with Brads but not that of Bud. Are you sure?"

Alan replied, "Yes. Bud told me himself. Neither of these guys were on the *Demson* when it went down. They were both off the boat to prepare for the wedding. Even Lil Brads had taken a trip with us but left to go prepare for the wedding of Bud and Cal's sister, Brad's daughter, Sis."

Bob said, "It would be good to know when the wedding will be."

Mike stood up and went to the door, "I'll find out."

As Mike left, Alan continued, "There seemed to be a bit of an edge on the schedule the last few days. We worked all night in the heavy rain to finish the loading sooner than we would have, but much later than planned."

Bob said, "The *Demson* wasn't making its quota per the schedule. The propeller accident, the coal shipment, a trip through the Keweenaw Peninsula, and the equipment delays all added to the schedule pressure."

Mike came back in the room and interrupted, "The wedding is scheduled for tomorrow."

The room was hushed. No one could believe their ears.

Rick said, "That tells it all."

Bob said, "He was rushing at all costs to make the wedding. He was desperate and threw the safety of himself and others out."

Mike said, "He took good men with him to the bottom of Lake Superior. It just doesn't make sense."

Alan said, "It makes perfect sense. There was a lot of pressure on Brads to be there for his family. Many times, his job as a sailor got in the way of important events and activities Brads simply missed. After a while, it was just the way it was. No remorse and no second thoughts."

Alan continued with his explanation, "This was going to be another one of those events missed, but each member of the family that sailed on the *Demson* made it clear how big of a deal it would be to miss this particular one. Brads thought he could manage the schedule to make it all work. He was close, but things went wrong. Finally, he knew he was way off track in his timing and didn't care about anything after he realized he would fail to be there for his family again. He wanted to be in the right place at the right time but simply couldn't pull it off."

Everyone in the room looked satisfied.

Brown stood up, "Alan, you are good to go."

Alan said, "Okay, but what about the other survivors and the families of the dead? What can we tell them, and when can we tell them?"

Bob said, "That is my job. I am not going to tell them everything, but enough to be creditable."

Alan said, "That doesn't seem honest. I think you should tell them the truth. There are no secrets. I don't think I can keep my feelings to myself."

Bob said, "Okay, I will do my best."

Alan asked, "When will you be done with the notifications?"

Bob said begrudgingly, "By the end of the day."

The other men began to write their reports as Alan left.

CHAPTER 41

REUNITE WITH THE SURVIVORS

Alan said, "Where are my crewmates,
the ones that survived?"

Alan walked out the door of the conference room and looked about. The room had a low hum from an air conditioner. The voices he heard were low from a half-dozen people at desks and standing in the aisles.

He saw Stevens and walked over to him. He was speaking on the phone to someone. Alan overheard him tell the person on the other end that *Demson* was lost and seventeen sailors went down with the ship. He saw Alan out of the corner of his eye and turned to him. He held up a finger as to say, "Wait a second and I will be finished."

Steven finished the conversation with, "We will know more as the investigation is concluded." The person on the other end asked a question. Steven replied, "The *Demson* was about fifty miles out from the Duluth break wall." Another question from the phone. Steven said, "I don't know why the *Demson* was out in the storm. We will know more later."

Stevens said, "Goodbye." He hung up the phone.

"Hi, Alan," Steven said cheerfully. "That was someone from the *Detroit Free Press*. They wanted some facts for their reporter. This is a very big deal around the country. I have talked to six or seven papers and the *AP Press* reporters. They are all sending someone here. I think the national television reporters are also coming."

Alan lurched, "Wow."

Stevens said, "They want to talk to survivors."

Alan said, "Where are my crewmates, the ones that survived?"

Stevens said, "They are all at the Willard Munger Inn. That is where I am going to take you."

Alan and Steven went out to the parking lot and got in a government truck with a Coast Guard emblem on its side. When Stevens started the truck, the radio was playing something by Three Dog Night. Alan had never heard the song. The idea of playing the radio on a lake freighter was impossible unless you were in port. Deckhands worked the lines while in port and didn't have an opportunity to tune in. The song that was playing Alan could relate to. "Mama told me not to come, that ain't no way to have fun."

The ride was simple and quick. Stevens and Alan got out of the truck. A group of reporters rushed toward them. They yelled, "Can you tell us about the tragedy of the *Demson*?"

Stevens held up his hand and said, "You must go to the Coast Guard Station for answers. Now let us through."

One reporter said, "You are from the Coast Guard, and you have brought nine people here from the station. They all look like survivors! We want answers!"

Stevens held up both of his hands as he backed up toward the hotel door with Alan in tow and said, "You must go to the Coast Guard Station for answers. Now let us go."

Once inside, the lobby was quiet. Alan, with Stevens's assistance, checked in. Alan became aware that he had no identification, money, or even a comb and toothbrush. He did have the knife he bought for Ham.

Alan asked, "How can I get some money for a comb and toothbrush?"

Stevens reached into his pocket and gave Alan two twenty-dollar bills. "Will this do?"

Alan said, "Thank you. Where are the others?"

Stevens said, "They are all together in adjoining rooms on this floor."

Alan said, "Thanks."

He went to his room and cleaned up. He then called room service for a burger and fries. As Alan waited for the food to come, he called the front desk and asked for the room numbers of his crewmates. Of course, they wouldn't tell him, so he went out into the hall and knocked on doors. He found all eight of the other men and Rosie.

Bobby gave Alan a big hug and said, "Thank you for taking care of me when I needed to find Rosie. All is well now."

Alan invited all eight others to his room. Most had eaten but a couple had not, and Alan called for room service for them. Rosie insisted that they all have steak and potatoes.

Alan said, "The investigation has concluded with each of us being interviewed. I think we are at the hotel in case there was more to be determined."

One of the licensed engineers said, "No, I don't think so. I think they are keeping a lid on us so we don't talk to the press or anyone else. I haven't called home yet. My family may not know I am even alive."

Bobby blurted, "Why are we guessing? Let's ask the Steel Company representative."

Rickie asked, "Do we know who he is?"

Alan pitched in and said, "Yes. He is Bob Carmichael."

Rosie and Bobby declared together, "We know Bob. He is a good man. Let's get him to talk with us."

The food came. The hungry ate and then they all talked about their ordeal.

When they we finished the food, they all went to the front desk and asked for Bob Carmichael. The front desk waved over to a man in the corner. It was Stevens.

Stevens came up to them and asked, "What's up?"

Alan said, "We would all like to talk to Bob Carmichael. We want to talk to our families and to go home."

Stevens said, "Sure. I'll call him."

Stevens went to a pay phone in the lobby and made a call. He talked for an inordinately long period of time. When he came back he said, "Bob is coming now."

It wasn't long, and Bob strode through the lobby door. He had a cheerful voice and said, "I am not very good at this and I am certainly sorry for the confusion. We haven't had a boat sink in a long time, and I am operating from a checklist created years ago. The press, the federal government, the families, and you are all different than the last time. Everything is faster. We didn't have survivors last time.

"Look, call home from your rooms. Tell your families you are alright. For those of you who want to leave, we will make arrangements for your departures tomorrow morning. For those of you who want to be placed on another boat, I will have the interviews with you and the potential captains tomorrow as well. That doesn't mean you can't go home for a while before reporting. How does that sound?"

Bobby asked, "Can Rosie and I be togetha' on the next boat?"

Bob said, "Of course."

Alan said, "How will a memorial be handled for the dead?"

Bob said, "I don't know yet. Something on the lake and you will all be invited at the Steel Company's expense."

Bob Carmichael then said, "Alan, we will mention your grandfather, Cap'n, as well."

Alan thought, *Did he know about the experience he had seeing Cap'n on the* Demson *just before the sinking?*

The engineers all wanted reassignments. So did Rosie, Bobby, and Rickie. The oiler, wiper, and Alan had enough. The simply wanted to go home. As they left the lobby, each one of them hugged and promised to see one another at the memorial.

Bobby asked Alan, "How did you do it? How did you know where to go and get to the aft end of the boat in time to get on the lifeboat with us? We barely made it ourselves, and we didn't have six hundred feet of steel and water to go through."

"I had help from the bosun mate. He told me where to go," Alan reverently uttered.

Bobby said, "C'mon. I don't think he liked you all that much and certainly didn't know his way around the boat." The other crewmates surrounded Alan. They were very interested in the story.

Alan said, "Look, the bosun mate at the end resembled my grandfather right down to his missing leg. I believe it was my Cap'n. Cap'n had been in a similar sinking in a 1913 storm. He had made his way through the inner passage on the non-buckling side of his boat too. He pointed me to the right way to go. You may not believe me, but it is true."

Bobby said, "I believe in spirts."

The other crew members nodded. One said, "I believe that could happen."

Alan said, "Okay. It is off my chest."

The crew members departed and went to their rooms to make their calls.

CHAPTER 42

THE MISSED CALL HOME

Alan cried.

Alan dialed the phone number for his parents. No one picked up the phone. He tried again thinking he misdialed. No one was home. He then realized they were all at the funeral for Cap'n.

Alan cried.

He was missing one of the important family events that sailors miss. He was a sailor, at least for that summer. He thought that he paid his dues. Missing events, being in a tragic boat sinking accident, and losing friends were all part of his experience.

It all seemed sad. Alan composed himself and said out loud to no one in particular, "I will be okay."

He fell asleep and slept through the night.

Bob and Rick were up. They were not happy with the conclusion that the Steel Company and, in particular, that Brads was at fault. They both were insistent that the insurance company was the source of the blame.

Alan was a problem. Would he go home and be quiet, or would he continue to be a source of an alternative story?

CHAPTER 43

THE INTERACTION

*Hard Rock asked the first question,
"How did you survive?"*

Alan got up and showered and got dressed. Alan left his room to get some breakfast and some air. It has been a day and a half since the recovery of the crew.

He went outside and stood at the lobby door. A rush of media types came at him. Alan stood his ground. He remained motionless. He remained fearless.

Alan looked around, and in the bevy of reporters, he saw whom he recognized as Hard Rock. Alan grew angry. Why was Hard Rock here? He was left in port three hundred miles away. It made no sense. Alan knew he wasn't on the *Demson* because he saw Swing and his grandfather. Hard Rock took care of him, but in a manner that was abusive.

Hard Rock asked the first question, "How did you survive?"

Alan told of his trek through the inner passageway and how he leaped the incoming water and made it to the aft lifeboat.

Hard Rock asked again, "But how did you know to go down the port passageway?"

Alan asked back, "How do you know I went down the port side?"

Hard Rock indicated that someone told him. Alan leaped at the man and hit him with his shoulder. Alan took him to the ground and asked in a whisper, "You were there, weren't you?"

Hard Rock got up and left. He looked back as he moved toward the back of the parking lot. Hard Rock nodded his head as he caught Alan's eye. He mouthed the words, "Tell them what happened."

Alan turned to the assembly and asked, "What do you want to know?"

The only female reporter asked, "What happened?"

Alan told his story and that of the crew. He went through the propeller accident and the difficulty in closing the hatches. He mentioned the schedule conflicts with Captain Brads. Alan was honest. When Alan looked up, he saw Hard Rock was smiling. This was the first time he saw that bosun mate smile. It made Alan's day.

Within a few minutes, a car came screaming up to the lot of the hotel. Out bounded Bob and Rick. They pulled Alan back inside the hotel. Stevens had called Bob Carmichael and Captain Brown. Bob told Rick.

Rick said through his teeth, "I wished you hadn't told the press your story."

Bob added, "We are the spokespersons, and we have to contain what is said. You are not allowed to talk to the press at any time."

Alan said, "I told the truth."

Bob said, "It is not your place to speak for us. Your truth is from a guy that sees things and dead people."

Alan said, "You believe me, right? How do you know about Cap'n?"

Bob said, "No, I don't believe you, and therefore, I am not sure of your entire story. We are at loggerheads with what to say. I have spoken to all the crew and I know about your thoughts about Hard Rock, Swing, and the Cap'n. You need to shut up and go home."

Alan, shaken, said, "I saw what I saw, and they helped me through the accident. I am alive because of them."

Bob said, "We are helping you and you need to help us. The bottom line is liability. It means a lot—"

Alan retorted, "Of money."

Alan went upstairs and called home. Heard a click on the line. Alan didn't know but Bob and Rick were listening in.

Ham picked up, "Hello."

Alan softly said, "This is Alan."

Ham proudly said, "We are happy you are alive, and we are coming to get you. Grandpa's funeral was respectful with many guests. Your flowers arrived in time with a Steel Company representative in attendance. Real nice. We are now moving to your situation. Rap, me, and Elm will leave shortly and will be there in the morning. We saw you on TV, and we know this ordeal is tough on you."

Alan said, "I am getting some pressure to modify my story."

Ham said, "Don't do it. We'll see you tomorrow."

Ham hung up. Alan stayed on the line, and then after a few seconds, he heard another phone hanging up with a clunk and clink.

Rick said in another room in the Munger, "Bob, this is out of hand."

Bob replied, "Let's stop it now!"

· · · · · · · ● ● ● ● ● ● ● ● ● ● · · · ·

CHAPTER 44

THE SOLUTION

Alan moved to him and said, "Calm movements.
Take it slow and move your feet. Don't go under."

"Let's gather the crew and take them back out to the scene of the disaster," Rick said. "If we are going to get a sign-off on the propeller causing the sinking of the *Demson*, we need Alan and the others to agree with our facts."

Bob said, "Okay, but they don't trust us. You get paid if the story is right, and I get to save my company from liability and our reputation."

"Let's ask Brown and Stevens to arrange the trip out into Lake Superior!" decried Hamil.

The crew was alerted and assembled at the Coast Guard Station. They all boarded the *Woodrush* and headed out past the Duluth break wall in out into the lake. They covered the fifty miles to the point of the sinking in just a few hours.

Hamil pulled Alan and Bobby aside and worked on them to reset their stories. Alan and then Bobby refused. Bob took them to the top deck and had them lean over the rail to see if there could see anything of the *Demson*. It was a ploy.

Carmichael pushed them both out of the boat and into the water. He didn't say a thing, but only walked away. The water was not calm. The rise and fall of the waves were about five feet from top to bottom. Every once in a while, a white cap fell over the preceding wave. The skies were overcast which made everything seem colder. The water was very dark and ominous.

Alan was shocked as he hit the water. Bobby was not moving and began to sink. Alan grabbed him and pushed him up. Alan went under again. When he resurfaced, Bobby was moving. He was flailing his arms. Alan moved to him and said, "Calm movements. Take it slow and move your feet. Don't go under."

Lieutenant Brown caught sight of the two in the water as the cutter passed by. He ordered the wheelsman to come about as he ran out to the deck.

Back in Duluth, Ham, Rap, and Elm arrived at the Munger Inn. Rap went in and determined that all the remaining crew went to the Coast Guard Station.

He returned to the car and said, "Something's up. The surviving crew members were all moved to the Coast Guard Station. Let's go."

By the time the *Woodrush* was in position to rescue, two guardsmen went into the forty-degree water and a raft had been launched. The guardsmen were strong swimmers and pulled Bobby to the raft and pushed him up and into the vessel.

They turned to Alan who had cramped. Alan was under the water, and guardsmen didn't know exactly where he went under. They each dove and came back up empty-handed. Brown shouted for them to go out and away from the raft another thirty feet. Each swimmer went out and dove.

The first diver came back up empty-handed. He yelled, "He is lost! The water is cold and pulling us down."

After another fifteen seconds, up came the second driver with Alan in his arms. The other guardsman swam to both of them and helped bring Alan to the raft. They pushed him up and in. Bobby was spent but alert and yelled, "Alan!"

The guardsmen boarded the raft and began to give resuscitation. Alan was lifeless and blue. He had been under the water for a long time. The cold water slowed his metabolism and conserved his oxygen. As he warmed with the help of a blanket, he coughed and spit out an enormous volume of water.

The crews of the *Demson* and the *Woodrush* scampered to assist in getting the four sailors and the raft out of the water.

At the Coast Guard Station, Rap, Elm, and Ham went into the station. Rap demanded to know where the *Demson* crew members were. The Coast Guard personnel were not going to let anyone into the station.

"The media are supposed to stay out in the parking lot. Now get out of here," said a warrant officer. "Get out!"

Rap yelled back, "Wait a minute!" But as these words left his mouth, two guardsmen grabbed the three and pushed them out of the room.

"This isn't the way I envisioned this day starting," said Elm. "Let's go back to the hotel and call the station from Alan's room."

Back to the Munger Inn, the three went. The went inside and asked to use Alan's room. The clerk said, "He has been checked out just like all the others."

Ham was agitated, "Okay, can we use a phone?"

The clerk gestured to the pay phone in the corner of the lobby.

Elm asked for change. The clerk said, "We only supply coins to the paying guests."

Elm fumbled through her purse and found a quarter. Rap called the operator for a connection to the Coast Guard Station.

Now that the four sailors were back on board the *Woodrush*, Captain Brown asked everyone to join him the galley. "What happened?" asked Brown.

No one saw anything. Bob and Rick chipped in, "We think that the two were distraught from the interviews, and now being in the area of their dead friends and crew members, they snapped and went in after them."

Rosie cried, "No, that doesn't make any sense. Bobby loves life and me! I know Alan had been under pressure and talking about seeing dead relatives, but he never gave any of us the feeling of despair."

Back in Duluth, "This is the Coast Guard Station at Duluth, Minnesota. If you are calling about the *Demson*, please call Washington, DC, or the Steel Company in Cleveland, Ohio," stated the receptionist."

Rap said, "I want to speak to my friend, Brown, Captain Brown. Tell him Rap is calling."

"Captain Brown is out on patrol," the person on the line drawled on.

Rap said, "This is extremely important. Call him ship to shore."

"Okay, I will give you to the warrant officer," she answered.

"This is Warrant Officer McGill," Rap heard on the receiver.

Rap explained who he was and who the other two people the guardsmen threw out of the station. McGill apologized and said, "Come back to the station and we will get Brown on the line."

Hamil and Carmichael were desperate. They were being challenged by the *Demson* crew. How long could they keep everyone guessing and turn the room toward their story?

Carmichael bolted and grabbed the captain's weapon. He said, "Everyone, up on deck."

Hamil followed Carmichael's lead. He pushed everyone forward.

"Captain, order abandon ship!" yelled Carmichael. Brown was halting in his manner. Carmichael yelled again, "Abandon ship now!" Hamil hit Brown, and the captain fell to his knees.

Hamil said, "I am taking over this vessel. Now abandon ship!"

The engines came to a stop. There was silence. The wind was blowing gently. The sun was waning in the west.

Alan came to. He was groggy but alert. He got to his feet and off the bunk. Bobby was still but breathing heavily.

Alan staggered out of the bunk berth and stepped over the raised bulkhead. He could feel that the engines were stopped. He could also hear voices on deck.

Alan was aware that Bob Carmichael had pushed Bobby and him off the deck and into the water. He was alert that danger might be near. He moved up the stairs and entered the empty wheelhouse.

The phone rang, and immediately Alan answered the phone. "Ahoy?"

The person on the other end said, "Wait." He handed the phone to someone who said, "Hello, Alan, with us is Rap with your mom and dad."

Alan whispered, "Carmichael tried to kill Bobby and me by pushing us into Lake Superior at the spot where the *Demson* went down."

Rap said calmly, "Where is Carmichael?"

Alan replied, "I don't know, but it is quiet."

Just then, Hamil came in. "I thought I heard someone!" he yelled. "Let's go."

Alan dropped the phone but left the microphone open.

Alan was escorted down to the main deck with all the others.

Hamil said, "You have escaped death twice this week. I think a third time is a charm."

Out of the shadows bolted Hard Rock. He grabbed Hamil and threw him overboard. Carmichael shot Hard Rock three times before he went down in a heap. He ordered two guardsmen to toss him over the side as well.

Carmichael said, "Okay, abandon ship or I will push each one of you over just like I pushed Bobby and Alan. I wanted Alan's story to go away. The Steel Company will lose a fortune. But more importantly, Brads's reputation will stay intact. Lil would accept that he didn't make his commitments again, but she would not accept that he killed his crew to try to keep a promise made to her. I've known the Brads for a very long time and don't want that on their heads."

Alan shouted, "But you will do something worse! We are not the fault or the problem! We are simply honest, hardworking people."

Just then, Bobby appeared. He rushed Carmichael from behind. He lifted him up by hugging him from behind and walked him to the edge of the boat. He tossed the small man in.

Captain Brown ordered a rescue. Everyone was diligent and skillful and worked quickly. However, no one was saved or even recovered. The lake does not give up her dead.

CHAPTER 45

· · · · · · · · ● ● ● ● ● ● ● ● ● · · · ·

IT IS OVER

The Woodrush *got back to port a little before dawn.*

The crew made ready for the return to Duluth. The mood was just as somber as that voyage earlier that week.

Alan hummed, "Early in the evenin', just about suppertime, over by the courthouse, they're starting to unwind" (by Creedence Clearwater Revival).

The sky was finally clear, and all the stars the Swede and Alan saw so many days ago were out with a brilliance.

The *Woodrush* got back to port a little before dawn. The Coast Guard crew was released, and the *Demson* nine were told they could go home.

Captain Brown cleared the decks and took Alan to Ham. There were still reporters in the parking lot, but they stayed away and only spoke to the Coast Guard representative.

Alan rushed to Ham and gave him a big hug. "Great to see you," Alan cheerfully reported.

Ham said, "Me too."

Alan saw Elm and moved to her as well. "I am so happy to see you."

Elm said, "We were so worried."

Then there was Rap. Alan came up to him with hand out for a shake. Rap grabbed his hand and pulled him close. "You gave us a scare. We hung on that phone line and heard a few things, but then it went dead. We thought you were gone again."

Rap went on, "Then Captain Brown called us back. We were very relieved. We know all about Bob Carmichael and Rick Hamil. What a disappointment and tragedy."

Ham said, "The Steel Company, with a little help from Rap, had a check waiting for you in the Coast Guard office. We couldn't sign for it, but you can go in and get it before we take off."

Alan entered the station, and there were the *Demson* crew lined up to say goodbye. Alan began to well up. He hugged the engineers, oiler, and wiper. Then he said goodbye to Rickie. Finally, Rosie hugged him and said, "Thank you for saving our lives."

Alan said, "Thank you for being my friend."

Rosie said, "We are family now."

Bobby stepped in. He couldn't get the words out but said, "You're...ah...best."

Alan turned and repeated, "Thank you, all."

Captain Brown came up and said, "Here is your check for fifteen hundred dollars and some cents and a hearty send-off from the crew here at Duluth station."

Alan did a mental calculation and determined he was never paid for overtime even though he worked many long days, especially in port. Alan didn't care much. Alan signed for the check, shook the captain's hand, turned to go, and saw everyone in the building stand and give him an ovation. He was touched and left with a smile and tear.

As he came out of the station, Ham said, "Here are your things from your hotel room."

Alan said, "I really didn't have anything but clothes..."

Ham said, "And this knife."

Alan said, "I forgot. It is the only thing I saved form the *Demson*. I bought it for you, Dad."

Ham said, "I remember. Something about the replacement for the samurai sword I have from the war."

"Yes," Alan said softly.

Ham said encouragingly, "We can sort it out when we get home, but I completely understand the thought."

"By the way," Elm softly inserted, "do you remember Charlie, who was a patient at the county hospital where Cap'n spent his final days? The nursing staff said that you came by his room on your way to see your grandfather."

Alan explained, "It was an accident. I couldn't see the number of the room without stepping inside. I am sorry, but I was looking for Cap'n's room."

Elm patted Alan's hand. She continued, "Oh no, as it turns out, it was a very good chance connection. Charlie apparently spoke about you often after your visit. He was concerned about your safety this summer on the lakes. Just before he died, about thirty minutes after Cap'n, he said it would be all right for you."

Alan's inquiry had a sense of foreboding, "He is dead? I didn't even tell him I was working on a boat this summer. The freighter experience was a topic we never spoke about. I was with him just a couple of minutes."

Elm went on, "Oh, he knew somehow. He was anxious for you and painted a picture for you. Although he was a quadriplegic, he could masterfully paint with his mouth."

Alan explained, "I know. I saw his work. He broke his neck while swimming at the bridge just before our third-grade fall class began. Our teacher told us of the tragedy. I saw his water-based themes depicted in water colors all over the walls in his room. Some pictures were scary."

Elm pulled from the car a framed picture for Alan. Alan took the picture and looked at the composition. He dropped the picture in horror.

None of his three relatives understood. Ham asked, "What is the deal, Alan?"

Rap asked, "Why in the world are you acting this way?"

Elm said, "I know why this is so difficult. It is about your experience, right?"

Alan picked up the art and showed the three of them. "It is a picture of Brads in the wheelhouse, near the end of the ordeal of the

Demson sinking. Just before I jumped into Lake Superior next to the flailing lifeboat, I looked up and he was watching me. He smiled and waved though the wind, rain, and waves. The picture showed Charlie standing, not lying down, a little behind Brads and to his left. Charlie captured the scene just as Alan saw it with all the environmental torment and the glory of the captain at peace. Charlie captured the ghostlike essence of light and serenity surrounding Brads and him, just as I witnessed in Charlie's room when I stumbled in."

Elm reverently said, "Charlie died just before the *Demson* sunk but captured it in this painting a few days before it happen. The nurses said he wanted you to have it. He said you would be alright and understand."

Alan wept.

He was ready to go home.

· · · · · · · · ●●●● ● ●●●● · · · · · ·

CHAPTER 46

THE RIDE HOME

Everyone in the car but Alan was singing along. Alan
didn't know the song. He was happy to be back.

Alan and the three members of his family got in the '66 Bel Air. It needed gas, so Ham said, "Let's get some gas and drinks for the road."

As they pulled into a Sinclair gas station, Alan noticed the dinosaur mascot logo in the window. It was great to be going home and permanently on land again. He noticed when he shut his eyes he could still feel the movement of the water.

As the attendant filled the tank, Ham went into the station. Ham came out with four cans of Vernors Ginger Ale. Ham paid for the gas and then drove off.

Elm said, "It is a long drive. So we planned to stop at the Tahquamenon Falls in Paradise and spend the night. From there, we will go down and over the Mackinaw Bridge and spend some time exploring. This is where we will spend the night. Finally, the next day we will stop at the Wilson Cheese Shop in Pinconning, then Frankenmuth, for dinner and then on home."

Alan said, "That sounds great, but let's stop at Emil's for Buffalo Burgers instead of Frankenmuth."

Everyone agreed and then moved into the conversations about Cap'n's funeral and Alan's ordeal.

The ride was delightful. When the conversation was spent, Ham turned on the radio to country and western station. Playing was, "Hello, darlin', nice to see you. It's been a long time. You're just as lovely as you used to be." It was Conway Twitty singing. Everyone in the car but Alan was singing along. Alan didn't know the song. He was happy to be back.

After the two-day trip, everyone was happy to be home. Ham paid for everything, and Alan knew that it was a big burden on the family.

Alan said to Ham, "I have been paid almost sixteen hundred dollars for the summer. Can I pay for anything?"

Ham said, "No, pay for your education. This was our vacation, and we brought our son home."

CHAPTER 47

· · · · · · · · · ● ● · · · · · · · ·

THE FINAL CALL

"Hi, Alan. This is Lil, Lil Brads."

When Alan walked into his home, Carol and Bert welcomed him home.

Carol said, "It is good to see you."

Bert said, "I have to give up my bedroom again."

The phone rang, and Elm answered the call, "Hello."

Someone spoke on the other end.

Elm said, "It is for you, Alan."

Alan took the receiver and said meekly, "Hello."

"Hi, Alan. This is Lil, Lil Brads."

Alan was flabbergasted. "Hi, how are you?"

Lil began, "I know this is out of the blue, but I wanted to call and thank you. You had the courage to explain the last couple of days of my husband's life. I couldn't figure out what he was thinking. I was angry with him. I just couldn't answer my questions until you pieced everything together.

"Cal was so unhappy. Bud was excited. And my captain was trying to fulfill my wishes. He tried until the end. I know now that he was trying to make the wedding, but simply couldn't. He killed himself trying and took many others along with him in his effort. I am not sure how this will be viewed in the long run, but I know he loved us and tried to make us happy. For that, thank you."

208

Alan said, "It's alright. I want to thank you for the call. It means a lot."

Lil said in passing, "By the way, two strangers came to the wedding. A man wearing an army dress uniform, helping a one-legged man, in a Steel Company uniform. They came in late. They sat in the back and, without a word, disappeared as the last words of the ceremony were uttered."

Alan asked, "Was it the left leg?"

Lil asked, "What?"

Alan asked again, "Was the missing leg of the Steel Company officer his left leg?"

Lil simply said, "Yes, yes, it was. Why?"

Alan said, "Thanks. I think they were people I knew. But who knows?"

Lil said, "Well, Alan take care. Goodbye."

Alan hung up.

Elm and Ham asked, "Who was that?"

Alan said, "It was Lil Brads. She thanked me for being so honest. She also said that Hard Rock and Cap'n attended her daughter's wedding."

· · · · · · · · ● · · · · · · · ·

CHAPTER 48

THE MEMORIAL

Bobby looked to Alan with wonder in his eyes.

It was almost a year ago when the *Demson* went down. Alan has moved through his sophomore year of engineering school with outstanding grades. There isn't a day that Alan doesn't recall something about his summer on the *Demson*.

He loves the long, sleek nature of the ore boats. He knows that he will never sail again, not because he was afraid of the blue-black water but because he doesn't want the lifestyle. He wants to be around for his future family events as much as possible. He certainly doesn't want to miss his daughter's wedding if he gets married and has children someday.

He is on his way to Duluth by car. This time, he is alone. Ham and Elm are busy working. He is retracing the trip across the Mackinaw Bridge and through the Upper Peninsula of Michigan. It will take two days, and because it is over the weekend, he won't miss work at the summer factory job he acquired. He will miss the overtime opportunity the union job afforded.

"Joy to the World" by the Three Dog Night was playing as he made his way to Duluth. "Jeremiah was a bullfrog, was a good friend of mine. Never understood a single word he said, but I helped him drink his wine."

He arrived in Duluth, and the Steel Company had rooms for the nine sailors in the Munger Inn. The memorial will be on the shore near the break wall.

As Alan arrived, he saw Bobby and Rosie. They came to him and everyone hugged.

Alan said, "It is good to see you both. What are you doing these days?"

Bobby said, "We went back to work for the Steel Company right away last year. We were able to be assigned on the same boat, but not in the same roles. I am assistant cook and Rosie is a steward."

Rosie said, "It is okay, but not what we would have hoped for. There is not much movement in the cook and steward ranks, and we needed to be accepted by a new captain. With all the events of last season, we are a bit tainted."

Alan said, "Oh, I am sorry."

Bobby said, "No need. How are you?"

Alan said, "Well, I am really sorry for you and how things have gone."

Changing pace, Alan went on, "This summer, I work in a factory. It pays well with overtime at time and a half, but it's not my last job. I am okay."

Rosie inquired, "You still in engineering school?"

Alan replied hopefully, "Yes. I am now going into my junior year this fall. Still an engineer."

"Have you seen anyone else?" Bobby asked.

"No, not yet, "Alan replied. "Let's go ask."

The three approached the desk clerk, the same one as last summer. Rosie braved, "Are any of the *Demson* nine survivors here yet?"

The clerk said pleasantly, "Yes, they are waiting for you in the dining room."

The three travelers strode across the lobby and into the hall to the dining room. They entered the room and were met with laughter, hugs, and hellos. The mood was light and airy. Everyone was happy to see one another.

As Alan was taking note, he noticed that Rickie wasn't there.

Alan declared, "Where's Rickie?"

Bobby asked, "You didn't know? He didn't get a job after our incident and went home. He didn't have any money after a few weeks and stole food to eat. He was caught, of course. He was arrested and put in jail for ninety days. When he got out, he applied to get on with a cook crew. But now he had a record and was done. He is working on a farm in Georgia and simply couldn't make it."

Alan said, "I miss him."

"As do we all," Rosie replied. "Now let's have some fun and remember our dead."

They ate dinner with a couple of Steel Company officials. None of the men were known to any of the crew. They had a good time and told some jokes.

Alan told a joke about whales. "Whales don't go into the Caribbean Sea. Whales have wide flares at the end of their tails called a fluke. So if you see a whale diving in the Caribbean, it is a fluke." No one got it. Then Alan explained it, and everyone politely laughed.

The oiler said, "It sounds like a joke my dad would tell." Everyone laughed, hard and long.

The night aged and everyone went to bed.

The next day, they were up and at breakfast by eight. After eating eggs with bacon and pancakes, Alan went outside. The day was clear and cool, but quite breezy.

A bus came to pick them up and take them over to the station for the memorial. As they got on, the bus driver said good morning to everyone but Alan, Rosie, and Bobby. All three noticed but didn't make anything of it.

As the bus arrived, the driver helped almost everyone off but didn't wait for Alan, Rosie, and Bobby to get off before going into the station. This time, the three not only noticed but were also concerned. They were upset. What was the problem with the driver?

As Alan approached the station, he could see many townsfolk, reporters, and family members in attendance and wearing name tags with their affiliation.

There were many conversations underway. The mood was optimistic, but solemn.

Captain Brown and Lieutenant Stevens were leading the group to their memorial seats, and the dais was set with chairs for dignitaries. The raised platform had a Steel Company flag on one side, a United States flag in the center, and a Coast Guard flag on the other side.

The driver of the bus came to Alan and said, "I am a nationalist and have some trouble with you sitting with those black couple."

Alan said, "You are so out of line. Bobby saved the rest of us. He is a hero. I am so embarrassed by your unwitting insult. Get away from me!"

The driver recanted and said, "I didn't know. I am sorry."

Alan shouted, "Don't say you're sorry to me! Say it to them." He pointed to Rosie and Bobby.

The driver went to them and said, "I'm sorry" and rushed away.

Bobby looked to Alan with wonder in his eyes.

Rosie mouthed, "Thank you."

The assembly moved to the chairs, and the dignitaries took their places. The wind was blowing the hair, clothing, and papers the people on stage were holding. Alan saw Lil in the front row. She was with Cal. She looked well and dressed appropriately for the occasion.

The ceremony contained singing of the national anthem, a prayer by a chaplain, and a verse from the Holy Bible about the sea, Psalm 107:29, "He caused the storm to be still. So the waves of the sea were hushed." The wind dropped at that moment.

Then there was an opportunity for the Steel Company to speak about the men and women of the *Demson*. They were artful, and the messages were of heroes, hardworking skilled sailors, and the brave.

Then with a pause, they gave Cap'n a special recognition.

At the end, they addressed the living. They wanted everyone to know how grateful they were for the lives of their loved ones and those that survived the ordeal. They were thankful for their efforts.

Alan rose humbly without saying anything. The crowd noticed him, and eventually the Steel Company officers did as well.

Alan remained silent. Then Captain Brown stood and asked Alan if he had anything to say.

Alan started, "I, we, truly appreciate the memorial." He let that rest. He moved slowly to, "I have a couple of requests. I would like to suggest that the cooks and stewards from the *Demson* be placed as a team back on one of your boats immediately. They deserve that courtesy and respect."

Alan went on, "I would also like the other members of the crew to be given an opportunity to help improve the policies of the Steel Company. I think that the length of time from 1913 to 1970 would have been sufficient to put in place better safety practices which could improve the chances of the crew, especially in the forward cabins, surviving an abandon ship order. I, for one, would welcome the chance to help. Finally, I would like the families of those that were lost on the *Demson* be given a place that they could go to visit and remember their loved ones."

Alan sheepishly smiled and retorted, "Oh, I forgot. The overtime policies involving deckhands and others are inappropriate. The men and women work many long hours and, on Sundays, when in port or going through the Soo, with limited time off as compensation or with limited overtime pay. This practice should be reviewed. It seems unfair."

The Steel Company officers looked helpless. They were taken off guard. But then with composure, one of the Steel Company officials said, "We will take these issues under advisement."

Lil Brads stood. Then other members of the audience representing the dead crew families stood. Then all the remaining memorial attendees stood.

Lil said respectfully but defiantly, "No. No, tell us now!"

The crowd began to shout, "Tell us now! Tell us now!"

Finally, Captain Brown took the stage and put up his hand to quiet the crowd. The chatter went on for another twenty seconds or so. The assembly finally quieted and sat down. The only sound was that of the wind and waves in the background.

Captain Brown looked at the Steel Company men on stage and said, "Tell us now." The crowd was absolutely stunned, and then after the comment was taken in, the murmur of chatter between friends became a roar of delight.

Captain Brown again raised his hands for quiet. He looked at the company men and asked gently, "Well?"

One, then another and another rose until they all stood up and huddled with their backs to the audience and conferred. Then they turned to the crowd and one said, "We agree to everything Alan has asked for on behalf of the *Demson* crews and families. Everything!" He paused, looked at Alan, and asked respectfully, "We only ask that Alan help us figure out the process and delivery on this commitment."

The crowd cheered. It was thunderous. It was elevating. Captain Brown's smile broadened to a grin.

Alan went to the stage. He calmed the crowd and said, "Thank you all, and you gentlemen who represent the company as well. But I can't accept your offer to have me be the only helper and point person on this important task. I live in Michigan, and your offices are in Ohio. I'm a student, and I must return to engineering school."

Then without hesitation, he immediately said, "I would ask you to consider Mrs. Brads to be our point person. She lives close to you, and I believe she is very capable. She can reach out to all of us, and we can help her as we are needed."

Alan asked Lil, "Will you accept our request to represent us?"

Lil looked up and said with tears in her eyes, "Yes, yes, I will."

The day came to an end. The *Demson* families and crew members said goodbye.

Cal found Alan and hugged him. "You are the best, man!"

Alan said, "Good luck. Say hi to Bud and… ah…Sis, of course."

Cal replied, "I will."

Then he said almost in a whisper, "Bud took the compass."

Alan looked a Cal with a glare that was piercing right through him.

Alan gritted his teeth and got out, "Ouch! Dag nab it, he nearly killed us."

Cal said carefully, "He paid his dues with the company. He confessed. He was held accountable."

Alan thought about it. He said, "Okay. Why didn't we know about any of this until now?"

Cal said tenderly, "My mom prevailed with the officials and lawyers to not have another family member placed in a position of distress. There is a confidentiality agreement. Given the dire outcome of this action and its effects during the sinking of the *Demson*, she will work hard on this issue as well as the other items committed to by the Steel Company. It is her chance to make amends for the part she and our family played in tragic events that unfolded."

Alan said, "Okay. All right. Good luck and return safely home."

Alan got in his black Studebaker Lark and drove off with the windows down and radio up. The Beatles were singing, "It has been a hard day's night, and I been working like a dog. It's been a hard day's night, I should be sleeping like a log."

EPILOGUE

*The degree Alan would earn would
be his achievement alone.*

The drive home was like a reset. Alan would enter his junior year of engineering school. The draft was over as the reckless and confusing war in Southeast Asia was no longer being pursued. The world was on the verge of tremendous economic struggles and extremely high interest rates.

The degree Alan would earn would be his achievement alone. Others would contribute, but no one else was the big benefactor that made a huge difference in the outcome.

The adventure of Alan's life was just beginning, and there would be many more mysteries and stories to unravel over time. Alan loves the quote from Mark Twain, "The two most important days in your life are the day you were born and the day you find out why."

When Alan finally got home, he went to his room and turned on the radio. The song playing was "Operator" by Jim Croce. "Isn't that the way it goes? Well, let's forget all that and give me the number if you can find it so I can call to tell 'em I'm fine and to show I've overcome the blow. I've learned to take it well."

Alan said quietly, "I've learned to take it well."

QUOTES FROM MARK TWAIN ON LEADERSHIP

"The two most important days in your life are the day you were born and the day you find out why."

"You can't depend on your eyes when your imagination is out of focus."

"The secret of getting ahead is getting started."

Mark Twain lived from 1835 to 1910. He died a few years before the Demson was built. His real name was Clemens and was a writer, humorist, and lecturer.

QUOTES FROM WILL ROGERS ON LEADERSHIP

"Always drink upstream from the herd."

"Even if you're on the right track, you'll get run over if you just sit there."

"If you want to know how a man stands, go among the people who are in the same business."

"Try to live your life so that you wouldn't be afraid to sell the family parrot to the town gossip."

Will Rogers lived from 1879 to 1935. He died a few years before World War II in a plane crash in Alaska. He was an actor, humorist, and newspaper columnist.

LEADERSHIP PRINCIPLES: PERSONAL AWARENESS

(Found in the Story of the Sinking of the *C. M. Demson*)

Perfection is not a measure of success.

Integration of your life with work and family needs are essential.

Later in life, your marginal actions may be unacceptable to even you.

Even your worst actions should be available for primetime television.

Moral adherence is a crucial part of how to conduct all activity.

Mentoring helps.

Take care of yourself physically and emotionally.

A healthy lifestyle is extremely important.

Dreams can come true.

LEADERSHIP PRINCIPLES: ATTENTION TO OTHERS

(Found in the Story of the Sinking of the *C. M. Demson*)

Nothing is a secret.

It is your responsibility to prepare yourself and your team for the challenges at hand.

Depend upon your team, friends, and family.

You can be successful with the team you have.

Be transparent in your communication always.

Hard as it seems, people want to know what is changing and how it will affect them.

All people, no matter how they contract for their services, are full partners in the outcomes of their collective mission.

All people have the right to be heard and the requirement to ask for change in a civil manner.

Despite all the challenges and important activities around you, it is important to recheck your purpose to ensure its enduring nature.

LEADERSHIP PRINCIPLES: PLAN AND RESULTS

(Found in the Story of the Sinking of the *C. M. Demson*)

Ideas are not a plan, but they do provide direction.

Being in the right place at the right time happens when you prepare.

Work on a plan with your purpose in mind.

It is your responsibility to determine a plan that will meet your desired outcome.

There is always as yes to any question offered, but many times there must be a modification to achieve it.

Working hard and staying the course is rewarding.

Distractions are always at hand; therefore, do not lose focus as to what you are aiming to do.

Prepare at many levels for the variable outcomes that might occur.

Be flexible.

LEADERSHIP PRINCIPLES: WIDE-VIEW AWARENESS

(Found in the Story of the Sinking of the *C. M. Demson*)

What you do will affect your family, your leadership vision, and vitality.

It is important to understand how global, national, state, and local activity will affect your specific undertaking.

Be involved with the community to your capability.

Be current and advocate for your position.

The trends of the activity around you will create a future that is both understandable and predictable.

Not deciding on a course of action too quickly is sometimes the best choice.

You are always behind the technology curve, but technology is an important investment to your success.

Don't break the law.

Don't think you can make something illegal somehow to become legal.

LEADERSHIP PRINCIPLES: EXERCISE

(Found in the Story of the Sinking of the *C. M. Demson*)

There are four subtitle categories associated with the leadership principles. They are personal awareness, attention to others, plan and results, and wide-view awareness. All these four can be traced to, but are a modified adaption from, Robert E. Quinn's work on fundamental leadership questions at the University of Michigan.

There are ten principles per category. The categories can each be assigned a color, and a deck of cards can be created using all forty principles.

The cards are used in a group setting, passing out all the cards to the participants. If there are more than twenty people, use more than one deck. Each person takes a few minutes and exchanges cards with one another one at a time until the person has the cards that seem to fit for them.

The person then identifies their position on the quadrant where they see their cards placing them.

Each person then tells a story about their best when they used the principles from the cards they hold and the quadrant they have identified.

Then a discussion can ensue about why they chose the cards they did and how then could strengthen their leadership if they could work in every quadrant. What would it feel like if all principles were equally adopted?

Leadership Principles

	People Aware	Society Aware
Attention to Others		Wide-View Awareness
Personal Awareness		Plan and Results

Externally Sensitive

Internally Capable

"Bridge Over Troubled Water"—Simon and Garfunkel

"The Fightin' Side on Me"—Merle Haggard

"Wadhams" – Alan

"Mary Had a Little Lamb"—Thomas Edison

"Hey Jude"—The Beatles

"Black Magic Woman"—Santana

"Daddy Sang Bass"—Johnny Cash

"In the Summertime"—Mongo Jerry

"The Boxer"—Simon and Garfunkel

"That Ain't No Way to Have Fun"—Three Dog Night

"Willy and the Poor Boys"—Creedence Clearwater Revival

"Hello Darlin'"—Conway Twitty

"Joy to the World"—Three Dog Night

"Star-Spangled Banner" (national anthem)—Francis Scott Key

"It's Been a Hard Day's Night"—The Beatles

[A}Wad [C]hams, [B]Wad [A]hams. [A]Scoo [G]bee, [A]Doo [G] bee, [C]Doo [A]bee, [F]Doo.

[A}Wad [C]hams, [B]Wad [A]hams. [A]Scoo [G]bee, [A]Doo [G] bee, [C]Doo [A]bee, [A]Doo.

[C]We [D]have [E]a [F]school [F]and [G]a [A]gen [G]er [A]al [F] store.

[C]We [D]have [E]a [F]church, [G]who [A]could [G]ask [A]for [F] more.

[A}Wad [C]hams, [B]Wad [A]hams. [A]Scoo [G]bee, [A]Doo [G] bee, [C]Doo [A]bee, [A]Doo.

MY ACTUAL LETTERS HOME
IN THE SUMMER OF 1970
A BRIEF ANALYSIS

I was eighteen and had never been away from home. I would often say that I missed everyone at home and wanted to be there. These were the lamentations of a scared and less-than-confident kid.

I wanted to please my parents and certainly not let them down. I wanted to stay within their expectations, including moral attentiveness and, of course, laundry.

It was great that my parents came to see me. Their time was precious in getting time off from work, and I told them how much I appreciated it.

The work hours were scattered, and I wanted the people at home to know that it was difficult. I worked hard. It was probably good that I could write it down and tell someone of my perceived hardship. The weather was always important as we worked outside and on the water.

I got promoted twice throughout the summer. It seems like attrition helped now that I look back, but I knew at the time I was learning and growing. I was trusted.

The thought of making fifteen hundred dollars was outside my ability to imagine. I seemed to boast about making $2.42 to $2.55 an hour. It was a big deal to me.

The letter writing reflected my state of being and ability. Not my best skill but I did experiment with surprise and anticipation. I used slang, and I seemed to have a quite negative outlook. The names don't ring any bells after all these years, but they certainly seemed important to me at the time.

I asked for my father's praise and wanted him to write. Baseball was even a big deal on board a lake freighter. My mother and others wrote to me. With phone calls and waves from my friends and family at the Blue Water Bridge, I was happier.

I looked for connections, including friends, siblings, and grand-fathers. I wanted to know where I was going and when. It is good to reread all the city ports that I visited and worked.

I seemed overly directive, for example, when I told my dad what car he should buy. Planning was a skill I had even then, for example, when I wanted to plan on how I would get home.

I did get ringing in my ears or tinnitus while working on the boat that summer, primarily from hammering on steel bulkheads to chip away the paint without ear protection. It simply wasn't supplied. I still have the issue to this day.

The letters are a good connection with reality and provide a backdrop to the essence of the story of Alan and the *Demson*.

Postmarked June 9

Hi Mom and Dad,

Well its Monday and work is done for today.

The boat got delayed with unloading and we didn't leave Gary until 2:30 AM this morning. We, (myself and Jim (the Boson) and the other two deckhands, Chuck and Dan), had to close the hatches. It took until 4:15 A.M., I then got cleaned up at 7:30 A.M. and worked to wash her ship down. We worked all morning on the job, (had to do a good job, the old man's wife is coming aboard).

We only worked an hour and a half this afternoon, (I slept), because I worked last night, we sanded a door.

Overall, I like the people and the ship and the work.

At 2 or 3 tomorrow morning we will go under the Mackinaw Bridge, then we'll go to Two Harbors.

We have TV and stereo. All the modern pleasures of life.

I am well, but I miss home a little.

Love, Ron

*****

Postmarked June 12

Hi, Mom and Dad and Robbie and Cindy,

Well, we went through the Soo on Tuesday and got up to Two Harbors last night. We were called up at 8:00 PM and worked until 4:00 AM the next morning (this morning). It rained most of the night, and it was very cold.

One of the deckhands, Dan, was always messing around, not doing his share of the work. He messed up too often. Cap'n fired him. Chuck and I were shifting, and when we went to go to bed at four this morning, we found that when Dan had packed to leave, and he left the porthole open. Needless to say, the place was flooded. After work today, we had to clean up.

I did bring a Bible, my little black pocket one. Don't worry, Mom, I pray for you too. With prayer, anything can happen.

I love all of you.

Tomorrow we'll go through the Soo at 3:00 PM.

Love, Ron

*****

Dear Mom and Dad,

Hi! What a time! I've been tired all week. I barely get enough sleep to go on. Monday, we started on these hatch combings. The combing are about three feet high, and a sliding lid is placed on top. Well, here I am, hanging over the side scrubbing. The arms I have were worn-out the first day. The next two days, I don't know how I managed.

One of those days we went through the Soo was that terrible. We worked eight hours hard! And then we had to work hard at midnight to haul supplies. We fell into bed and then got up at 7:00 AM to start another day.

The weather's been fine, and I'm getting a small sunburn. It was eighty degrees in Duluth when we left there, and it's been nice ever since.

I am enclosing the first of my pictures for you. So keep watching. I miss you all.

Love, Ron

*****

Here it is, a week after I started, and I miss you more now than I did then. I guess seeing all of you under the bridge did it.

Today is Sunday and I read my Bible, John. There is no work today until about 3:00 PM. I get $3.35 an hour today. I figure I'll get about $120 a week.

It's pretty cool out this morning, plus I missed breakfast. I slept in.

I suppose today you will all take Cindy to State.

Robbie, school is out. You are now a big eighth grader. You'll have it pretty rough, doing the work of three.

The summer will go by pretty fast, and everyone will be back together again.

I don't like chipping. The hammer is still ringing in my ears.

I got to wash some clothes today. My supply is getting down.

I miss you all.

Ron

*****

Hi, folks,

These tickets are for Robbie to go putt-putting. I think they are still good.

Well, it's been two weeks, almost, and I'm not sorry I came sailing. Everything is going fine, but I'm a bit lonesome.

It is really foggy where I am on Lake Huron. We may have to anchor outside the Soo. If we don't, we'll go through at 4:00 AM tomorrow.

How was your trip to take Cindy over to State? Did Robbie Go?

Today I chipped all morning and painted all afternoon. Tomorrow we will finish the boat deck.

We had strawberries for dinner. It reminded me that ours should be on.

It is beginning to get cold, and I bet it is very cold in Lake Superior. We will probably go to Duluth. I don't think I have ever been there.

I miss you all very much.

Love, Ron

*****

Hi,

Boy, I would like to see you. When can you come? I would able to spend time with you in the down ports. I have to work solid in the upper ones.

The food is great. I think I am gaining weight.

It seems like I'm a big kid now when I see the people at the Soo looking at the show and I'm part of it.

Mom and Dad, I think of you a lot. I love you. I'm trying to be good.

I did my clothes the other day, but it didn't turn out like Mom's. I goofed someplace.

I worked all last night going through the Soo, and eight hours today painting. Tomorrow we go to Two Harbors at 7:30 AM. It is pretty hectic.

Love, Ron

*****

Dear Mom, Dad, and Rob,

How's everything? I would like to know about Grandpa's funeral. How was it? Were there many people there?

I would like to know when you are going to come and see me. I would like you to bring goodies with you.

What is Cindy's address? I want to write her.

Today on Lake Huron the wind was close to forty miles per hour. To make things worse, I was painting plus standing on a ladder, by the spar, by the pilot house.

Everything is going fine, and I think of you a lot.

The time sure is going by fast. I get a payday Sunday already!

It should be cold tonight, and we are going through the Soo at ten.

The boat is rocking pretty bad. I don't think I'll get sick, but I do feel woozy.

We got held over in Conneaut for hours due to a pileup of boats (a lot of them), so we now get into port (lower) at Tuesday.

I miss you all.

Love, Ronnie

*****

Postmarked June 28

Hi!

How is the world been treating you? This boat is getting me down. Every time I turn around, I'm thinking about home. I really don't want to go home yet. I would just like it if I could just see you all.

It is noon. I had chop suey for lunch. The food is the best part of the boat. Well, tomorrow's the day. Payday. I really don't know how much I'll get. It should be over three hundred dollars. By the way, I don't know my bank account number. Do you think you could find it for me? The number will be on my bank book in my bed stand (the one with my clock on it).

I got a letter from Cindy, Dave, and Mrs. Conlon.

How has the old vacation coming along, without "two kids" bugging you all? It's probably pretty peaceful.

Today we are just painting again. We went through the Soo tonight, then on to Gary. We won't go under the Blue Water Bridge, but we will go under the Mackinaw. When we went to Duluth, I got to go on a bumboat. All the stuff was pretty expensive, so I didn't buy anything. I must be pretty cheap.

I miss you.

Love, Ron

*****

Hi, Mom and Dad,

How was your trip? I hope it was a vacation from work and not more work for you to do.

I'm glad you are coming to see me. You know what I like.

I will give you my check when you come so I won't have to send it through the mail. You see, I have to have my bankbook to send it in. I don't want to lose it.

I get both Saturday and Sunday off this week. The fourth is the reason.

I'm not doing too much else, just working. This working away from home isn't all it's cracked up to be.

I met a guy on here that's going to GMI. He wanted to know all about it. Of course, I told him to get accepted early. This he will do next spring.

There isn't anything I need from home. I am very glad you will come.

Well, lunch is over, so it's back to paint, paint, paint.

Hi, Dad. Can't you write?

Hi, Rob. Nice to hear from you.

Hi, Mom. You're great!

I love you all.

Love, Ron

*****

Postmarked July 9

Dear Mom and Dad,

Here it is, almost twenty-eight hours since I've seen you last! It seems like time goes faster than anything. Boy, it was great to have you come down to see me. I wish again time wouldn't have gone so fast.

When I left you, I went back to the boat. Went and changed my clothes and then sat on the deck until quarter after five. At that time, we shifted the boat. Then we closed some hatches and sat around some more. When I finally finished up and got to bed, it was 11:00 PM.

I was dead tired! It seemed like I just shut my eyes when it was 7:00 AM, bright and early. To get a little more shut-eye, I missed breakfast and got up at 10:00 to 8:00 AM.

This morning, I helped hose the deck down. This consists of shoveling, hosing, and straightening the hose. All in all, a three-man job lasting four hours. The morning is shot (picture of a revolver with a line coming out and the word *bang* at the end). This afternoon, I painted white over red lead I put on last week. This was done on the bulwark around the aft end.

For supper, I had veal. It was very good, and I gorged (seeing I had no breakfast). Yes, the food is great!

I think (I say think because everyone has their own idea), my guess, we'll be going through the Soo at noon Thursday. I don't know where after that. The company always changes their minds as to where the least foul up is.

I am glad you didn't go to Conneaut last week to find I would be in Lorrain. That would have been terrible.

I miss you all a good deal. I would really like to be home this very minute!

I love you all very much.

Love, Ron

*****

Hi.

This day was a bummer! I didn't get to bed until very late (2:30 AM) last night. We loaded ore in Two Harbors. It seemed like we would never get done. We worked and worked. First day would stop to shift, then we would shift the boat, then stop for water. It took us eight hours to load where it should take four hours. So because I was late in getting to bed, I was tired all day. I got up fifteen minutes to 8:00 AM. I didn't eat any breakfast. Then I am not only tired but also hungry.

I painted deck today, mostly lines for walkways. Quite a drag! After I finished painting, I helped Jim, the boatswain, take inventory. It all finished up with steak for dinner!

After supper, we had a fire and boat drill. What a farce! Here's how it goes: The word is passed during the day there is going to be a drill. After supper, everyone naturally goes and gets a life jacket on, and then we all go up on deck and "shoot the breeze." Finally, the alarm sounds. Ernie, the first mate, says, "Wait for me." (He does this every time; it's part of the drill.) One of the deck watches goes up and asks if there are any messages and then runs all over, yelling, "Fire fore and aft." I just stand doing nothing.

All in all, that was my day. We go through the Soo at 5:30 AM Sunday. It will be overtime. Then Monday at 6:00 AM, we go by Port Huron. At 10:30 PM Monday, we will be a Lorrain. I will call you from there.

I love you all. Your letters are received gratefully.

Love, Ron

*****

Hi, Mom.

We left Conneaut about 11:30 PM. As we were closing up, it started to rain very hard. I could see about ten feet in front of me. The water was flowing so hard it went over my book tops.

The day we were in Conneaut was interesting. One of the wipers quit, and Jim the Bosun was fired. He got drunk. He was put off at Detour today. The wheelsman, Tom, went on vacation, so everyone was moved up. I am now bull deckhand. Chuck moved up to deck watch.

Today we painted and chipped in the windless room. I also cleaned the windless. It is a big winch which hauls the anchor up and down.

We got a third mate in Detroit. We went through Detroit at 2:00 PM and Port Huron at 8:00 PM. No one was at the bridge, but I knew you thought I went through later at night.

Time is slow. I'll have to quit counting the days. I get paid in a week and a half. I think I get off in Detroit when I do.

The new deckhand's name is Pete. He sailed before, and he is a graduate of Kent State. They had all the killings last spring.

We are supposed to go to Duluth but always have a chance of getting changed to Two Harbors. I'd rather go to Duluth (bumboat).

I miss you and love you.

Ron

*****

Postmarked July 20

Hi, Mom and Dad.

We got to Duluth yesterday at 7:00 AM. That meant I and the other two deckhands had to get up at 6:30 AM. We stayed around there until 7:30 AM. That was hectic. Here's how it went. We got the hatches open, and then we were waiting around until we got down river to the dock. When we got there, it started to rain. Boy, did it rain! I was soaked before I got on the dock and had to stand there for three hours wet, waiting to shift. Another boat was in the spot we were supposed to be, and we were on pins and needles waiting for them to get out. I finally got a break and went and changed my clothes. (That reminds me, I've got clothes in the washer.) I put my rain gear on and went back out. The ore didn't run so well, so we were waiting more than shifting.

A lot of changes came about. Another wiper quit. So we now have two new wipers, both over thirty. It's funny the other two were teenagers. We've got another boatswain; his name is George. He doesn't like college kids, and he is tough (ha ha!). That's what he tells us.

Well, we started to close hatches at 5:00 PM, and it started to rain harder (it drizzled all day). We finished at 7:30 PM. I worked twelve hours (wow). We flipped a hatch cover in. That made George mad. I guess I'm not so good with him.

Tomorrow, about 5:00 AM, we will go through the Soo. I really can't be sure of this though because the water is rough (coming over the starboard side), and that might have a little effect.

Well, I love you both a lot, and I miss you.

Say hi to Robbie.

Love, Ron

*****

Postmarked July 24

Hi, Mom and Dad.

The week is going fast, and I will get paid Sunday. It will be a biggie, probably $500.

Today we left Gary at 8:30 AM. That was a twenty-four-hour delay there. There were two boats ahead of us.

I tried to call you, but the operator found it out of order, so I reported it. I'll call you next trip.

The day started at 5:00 AM today after working until 12:00 AM last night. We worked until 1:00 PM and then we were through. All we did was hose down, pretty boring.

I got my room painted black now. It's all right.

You should, or I, thank the church for the cookies? Should I send a letter to the church or what?

The boat is a drag, and I'm sick of it. I can't wait get home to see you all. I miss you all very much.

Will go through the Soo tomorrow after supper.

Love, Ron

*****

Hi, Mom and Dad.

I've been pretty busy. The whole boat is pretty unbelievable. The caliber of people on this boat are so low I hate to think about it. The people act stupid, and the boat is culturally in the gutter.

George, the new bosun, is a pretty rough character on the outside. He wants to be liked, and at first, he wasn't, but now he's coming around. He'll be fine.

I got paid the other day, $429. Not bad, eh? I now have six and a half weeks to go.

I wish you could come down and see me again. If you don't, I understand. I will call you this week.

Today we painted hatch combings. What a job! First, we scrub, then hose, then chipped and then paint. We are now getting into Duluth on Sunday and the Soo Monday at night.

Things are working out so well. I used to write all my letters on Sunday. Now I can't. I guess I'll have to let things slide a week. I don't think people will mind too much not getting any mail from me.

The way things look, I should be home the eighth of September. I could get off in Detroit on the mail boat for $3 and ride the train home. The boat goes in only nine or ten blocks away. I could get on a train there if Dad could get me passes. That's a long way in the future, but it's something to think about.

Robbie, how's the job? How much money did you make?

I love you and miss you.

Ron

*****

Postmarked July 31

Dear Mom and Dad,

I talked to you last night or this morning, and I was so glad to talk to you. Boy, I have only five and a half weeks left. You're right, time sure does fly.

After I talked to you, we might go to Toledo. I will be sure and call you. As it looks right now, we won't, so you'll know what happened. I am sending you the rest of my slides, so here they are! I had to pay a kid for these, and you'll have to figure out a way to look at them.

I went to bed after I was done using the phone. I was tired!

I miss you and love you, and I hope to see you shortly. Oh, I'm enclosing the note for the Missionary Circle.

Love, Ron

*****

Postmarked August 4

Hi, Mom and Dad.

Boy, have I a lot to tell you!

Let me start from our phone call. We went up Lake Huron to Detour. We got to Detour at 7:30 AM on Saturday. After we left there, it took us seven hours to go up the St. Marys River. This leg of my journey is supposed to be five hours long, but because of the fog the day before, the locks were closed. So on Saturday, there were fifteen boats lined up to go through.

That shot our day Saturday. But one more thing about Saturday, the first of August, I got a raise. I am now making $2.42 an hour. A twelve-cent raise. I am beginning to roll in the dough.

Well, Sunday, I was awakened at 7:30 AM. I am supposed to sleep in! The voice said we are going to go through the Keweenaw Waterway. I never heard of it. Well, it is here on the map [drawing of the Upper Peninsula with a line through the appendage]. It goes through the land. Boats only go up this about twice a season, and I was lucky. It's about eighty feet wide and just fits a boat. The scenery was fantastic, and we even went by Michigan Tech at Houghton. Dennis goes there. That was great!

Well, after that, we went on up to Duluth and got there Monday morning at 1:00 AM. We loaded her up in eight hours. It took until 9:00 AM. So I got my day in early. I went to bed and slept until 3:00 PM. I wrote eight letters and then ate. Now I got three to go.

I really miss you all.

Hi, Dad. How's things? I wish you would write!

Love, Ron

*****

Postmarked August 12

Dear Mom and Dad,

It is Tuesday. We got up to Duluth at 7:30 AM Monday morning, and it took us eight hours to get the job of loading done.

Last night I was really sick. I threw up about six times. When it came time to work, I was still sick. I was constipated and I had the cramps in my stomach. My head ached with much stress. I'm getting better. A few of the other guys on the boat are sick. It must have been something we ate. I didn't work today and got paid for it.

Tonight we'll go through the Soo. The time will be about 2:00 AM. I guess I will have to get up for that.

Tomorrow I don't have to work. It's a holiday, Seaman's Day. That will be okay.

The two Chucks are getting off down below, so I will get two new working mates.

I will become deck watch next time I get above. I will remain so until I get off.

I miss you and love you.

Your son, Ron

*****

Dear Mom and Dad,

I am now working as a deck watch. I am making $2.50 per hour and doing about half the work. I really enjoy it, but I'll be glad to get home.

I've decided to take only two more trips. That will make me coming home around the fourth or fifth of September. I figured it would be easier on everyone and my pocketbook if I got off below. If we go Lake Huron on that trip, I will get off going up in Detroit.

So you have two weeks to get me a pass for the train if we go Chicago that trip. I figure if I get off in Detroit someone can come and get me.

We went to Duluth and loaded. That is where I became a deck watch. I will be a deck watch until I get off.

We will be at the Soo at twelve midnight tonight (Tuesday) and I guess Lake Michigan from there.

I love you and miss you.

Ron

*****

Dear Mom and Dad,

I was so surprised at Lorrain that I still think it was a dream. I had such a good time talking to you. I wanted to go home with you, but I'll earn $250 this way. I went back and got my jacket. One of the guards told Frank, the steward, that they were there. When he came back, he told me.

I was really glad to see you under the bridge. It looked like everyone came down to see me. It made me feel good.

We are going to go through the Soo at 9:30 AM this morning. That will be on my first watch. This deck-watching thing is real easy. I like it. I wish I could have done this a month ago.

The picture is of a bird going into the boat. This was taken the day you came down.

I miss you all very much now that I've seen you again.

Love, Ron

*****

Dear Mom and Dad,

Well, here I am, a deck watch but on a different watch. I am now on the four-to-eight watch. I don't have to work with George anymore. I am so lucky.

We went through the Soo in fine style and headed on up to Duluth. When we got there, it was eight o'clock at night. I was then on the eight-to-twelve watch, so I sounded four straight hours. I then went to be and slept for four hours. I got back up and started the four-to-eight watch. All in all, this is like stealing my $2.50 per hour. I don't do anything (hardly). It gets kind of tiring in the morning, but sleeping in is worth it.

I have one more trip! I'm glad. I'm really anxious to get off. I really would have like to stay one more trip, but I don't think I could take it.

Well, Cindy should be home by the time you get this letter. I hope she did well on her exams. She doesn't have too long to rest up, for she will start student teaching right away, huh?

Randy will be gone in another month. That will be tough to get used to.

I think I will call you from Conneaut.

I miss and love you.

Ron

*****

Hi, Mom and Dad.

The days are getting shorter before my return. I want to say right off the bat I love you both very much, and if I've seemed ungrateful lately, I didn't mean to. I will come home the boy you want. I will try to be good, like I have been out here. I am going to keep regular hours, do things for you, and try very hard to get As (I want straight As this time).

It was nice to see you under the bridge and other places. Boy, everyone was there. I really wish I was too.

We're losing time going up, and it looks like I get in some time on Monday. I would like you to be there when I get into port. I think we'll go Lake Michigan this time, but I can't be certain.

Are we going to get a new car? I would be nice. I think the Duster is great!

I got paid yesterday. I have saved to date $1,595.17. Not bad! I'll get another $150 this week.

I'll get a chance to look around Duluth since we'll be there twenty-four hours or more.

I will send a telegram to tell you where and when if we go Lake Michigan. I will call if it is Lake Huron.

I love you.

Ron

*****

ABOUT THE AUTHOR

Ron May is a forty-year electric utility veteran. It is an industry with a vast array of equipment and systems to deliver this essential product. He rose through the ranks from engineer to executive vice president. He has background in fossil generation, nuclear power, electric and gas distribution, administration, information technology, and human side of leadership. His positive and forward-leaning approach to leadership is a hallmark of his career.

In pursuit of his engineering degree, he worked for a summer on a Great Lakes ore freighter. This was a legacy job where his grandfather and two uncles were sailors at the officer level, including captain and chief engineer. The experience left a permanent impression on May's ability to meet the challenges of life.

Ron May earned his engineering degree at the University of Michigan. He attended the Advance Management Program at Harvard and received an honorary decorate in engineering at the Oakland University. Ron has coauthored the book *Project Management for Experienced Project Managers*. He has also created a leadership course for engineers for upperclassmen and graduate-level students.

May's interests include consulting on culture change, teaching leadership, travel around the world, and family-focused activities.

CPSIA information can be obtained
at www.ICGtesting.com
Printed in the USA
LVHW012018171220
674450LV00022B/2555

9 781643 348117